A SELFLESS

KIT SPAYD

Copyright © 2023 Kit Spayd
All rights reserved
First Edition

Fulton Books
Meadville, PA

Published by Fulton Books 2023

Registration Number: TXu 2-338-731

ISBN 979-8-88731-501-0 (paperback)
ISBN 979-8-88731-502-7 (digital)

Printed in the United States of America

Dad, thanks for always being there for me and my wild ideas. Thank you for being one of my best friends in the world and never making me feel like my dreams can't come true!

Love you.

ACKNOWLEDGMENTS

I would like to take a minute and acknowledge the service members of our military, our frontline workers, mental health professionals, and the emergency responders within our communities who have shown us what it means to live a selfless life.

BELLE

"These people are reckless and are going to get someone seriously hurt one day. I need you to handle this, Belle. It's getting out of hand."

"I know, AJ. I will call Matt and Cory and let them know what happened, if they don't already know."

"Thanks, Belle."

"You are welcome, AJ."

Belle Grant was the human resources / public relations director for Cocala Fire Department. It did not pay much, but she really enjoyed doing the job. What female wouldn't? Her days were the same (come in, do some basic paperwork, do some filing and interviewing—you know, the typical HR duties).

The department consisted of eighteen paid firefighters/EMTs/paramedics—thirteen men and five women—and she had developed a bond with each one of them.

Belle was attractive for a thirty-nine-year-old woman with two kids, was extremely outgoing, and was not afraid to speak her mind. That was one of the reasons why the township council wanted her for this job. She had a way with easing rising tensions with the other paid fire department in town. She had worked for Cocala for almost six years now and had had to deal with some fun and not-so-fun things during that time.

Her first month was pretty rough, and she wasn't sure if she was going to continue to work there, but then she realized they needed her, and she couldn't let them down. Plus, "I took this job, so I need to understand what comes with it" was what she told herself. The department had a call come in at a home down the street from her house; it was so far gone, they lost the house. Two people were trapped, and three firefighters were injured (from both departments) while saving the two trapped. None of the injuries ended up being anything more than superficial, but it was enough to scare Belle into reconsidering if this was the right job for her.

When she came in the next day, Tom (one of the older firefighters) came to her office and asked if he could "just talk" about the call. For about an hour, he talked and Belle listened. She was so grateful he felt comfortable enough to come and speak with her since she had only been there for a month, which took a lot of trust on his part, and it was not lost on her. After Tom left, one by one, the firefighters came in to talk to Belle about the call and how they felt. From that day forward, Belle had a new respect for this job and knew what she dealt with was nothing compared to theirs, and if she had to be all that to them, then that was what she was.

She had no background in what she was hired to do, but she felt she was doing a respectable job, and they must have thought so since they kept her all these years. She was a widow of a little over two years, with two children, but seemed to have devoted herself to her kids, work, and volunteering.

Her life was finally getting back on the right path. Things were really looking up for them, and she did not think anything could really change that. However, over the next few years, things would pop up in her life that she never would dream of coming up, paths would be crossed that hadn't been in decades, lines will be blurred, and life as she knew it would become vastly different for her—actually, for everyone she had ever known and loved. Secrets would be revealed, hearts would be broken, and more buildings would burn.

CORY

Every male in the Richards family worked in the fire service. It was drilled in their heads and ran rapidly through their DNA that they were to be a firefighter. The Richards men had worked or volunteered at Barcher since its start.

Cory became the captain of the department five years ago when the two departments became paid departments, but he volunteered there and spent most of his life there growing up. He was a great asset to the department. At twenty-nine years old, he was very content being a paid firefighter; it gave him a sense of accomplishment. He was definitely easy on the eyes, and most everyone who met him liked him instantly. He was a charmer with the men and ladies. He loved being liked and liked to be in love.

"Barcher, Richards... Uh, no, pretty sure that's not what happened... Oh, really? And you would know that how? Were you there?... Yep, I am... Fine." Slamming the phone down, he cursed to himself, *Who in the hell is she? She sounds like a real treat. How do they stand her over there? This is gonna be fun. I can't wait to meet this chick. Callin' here flippin' out on me, thinking she has a clue. She pushes a pencil all day and files paperwork. All she sees are papercuts, I am sure.*

Cory was infuriated with the way this woman spoke to him and her tone and, well, everything about her, and he hadn't even met her yet. He figured he would get a shower since she would take half the day to get there anyway. *More papers to file and papercuts to get.* He laughed at his joke and went ahead to get a shower.

While showering, he couldn't help but replay the conversation over in his head. *Seriously, who was that chick? Just because the town council decided to put you in that position doesn't mean squat to me. You are with Cocala, not Barcher. We don't need anyone like that here. We definitely have it together. It's a shame they don't over there, and I am sure she isn't helping much.*

After about twenty-five minutes, he was finished and grabbed his towel and wrapped it around his waist. He headed out toward the door and had no idea what was waiting for him on the other side. He opened the door and was speechless for a second—only for a second though. *Is this her?* he asked himself. *Damn, okay. This might get interesting.* Little did Cory know just how interesting and quite complicated it was going to get.

CHAPTER 1

For years, the Cocala and Barcher fire departments had had a rivalry that just couldn't be explained. Belle was warned when she was first hired; therefore, she was a bit nervous and at the same time a little intrigued of this said rivalry.

Belle's first encounter with Barcher was a what you could say a not-so-pleasant one. Both departments had a call, and in the middle of the call, a fight broke out. An actual fistfight among grown men—between Cocala's assistant chief and two firefighters and Barcher's lieutenant and three firefighters. It was ridiculous and most certainly unacceptable on all accounts.

Belle, having the job she did, had the inglorious task of documenting everything and everyone. This included the ones at Barcher too, which she was not looking forward to. She did get a small knot in her gut thinking of having to go there, because it was the one thing she had not had to do yet since working at Cocala; most of her dealings were over email or a phone call. There had never been that much of an escalation before. She had never even stepped foot in their building, and now she knew she was going to have to go there and question the ones involved—even a few times. *Ugh* was all she thought. As she picked up the phone to call over there, she got super nervous. *Belle, get it together already. You are thirty-nine years old and have a career in a fire department.* Relax *already.* So she dialed the phone and waited for an answer—but hoped for a voice mail so she didn't have to speak to anyone.

"Hello, this is Isabelle Grant from Cocala Fire Department." She waited for a response. "Are you aware that your men started a fistfight today while both departments were on that call?... Yes, if you are available, I would like to come over and meet with you and possibly speak with the persons involved in the incident… Yes, today… Okay, thank you. I will be over there soon."

Well, he sounds pretty arrogant. I am not looking forward to this meeting, that's for sure. At least she was dressed very professionally today. She had on a pale-blue button-down top (with a lace cami underneath), a gray pleated skirt, and charcoal-colored heels. Her hair was half up in a twist behind, and she was looking the part today for sure. It was a beautifully mild day for February in Minser. She walked out to her car and headed to the other side of town.

She walked up to the door and knocked. No answer. She walked around the side of the building and knocked on that door, and still no answer. *This is frustrating. I just called here, and one of their captains, Cory Richards, answered the phone and told me he would be here. Obviously, he is not.* Belle was beyond frustrated at this point. She decided to walk around the backside of the building, where she found a propped-open door.

She entered and called out, "Hello. Anyone here?" She looked around, and it seemed empty, but she knew someone had to be here—unless they just went around leaving doors open. "Hello." Walking around the engine bay, she took notice of the names above the lockers and their gear. She noticed the flags hanging above on the walls and the training board, and she saw *Richards. Hmm, that was who I spoke to on the phone a few minutes ago.* His helmet was pretty beat up, and his gear seemed very discolored. *I wonder what he has seen*, she thought to herself. She walked around a bit more and saw a room off to the right with bunks in it, a room with the door closed just past that, and a few more rooms and offices on the left.

Okay, this is ridiculous. Fifteen minutes I have been here, and nothing. Not one person. I am not waiting around for this and wasting my day. I will just send an email to his chief and AJ at council. Belle was already in a bad mood, so this did not make matters any better.

Both individuals blamed the other department for the fight and that it was escalated in her actually coming here to confront this like adults.

What an arrogant jerk. Who is he to tell me what I do and do not know?

A SELFLESS LIFE

What a piece of work. Wow, how do they deal with her there? I was talking to her for three minutes and already dislike her.

Just as Belle was getting ready to walk out, the door to the room she had just walked past opened, and *Wow* was all she could muster in her mind. Standing in front of her was one of the best-looking men she had ever laid eyes on, and she was married to one good-looking guy and worked with quite a few others.

He was in just a towel—a towel—that was wrapped around his waist and knotted at the side. The water was still dripping down over his chest and along his arms, and his hair was a disheveled mess. The way he glistened reminded her of when a sun-shower would occur and how the flowers and grass looked just after. She knew he could see how uncomfortable she was, and he somewhat enjoyed it.

Wow was what she wanted to say, but she settled for "Hi, I am Isabelle Grant from Cocala. I am looking for Cory Richards. Would you happen to know if he is here?"

Why is he just standing there staring at me?

"So can you tell me?" asked Belle.

"Yeah, uh, that would be me," Cory replied as he did a side grin, which, of course, made her melt even more. Her heart fluttered at the sound of his voice and the way smiled when he answered. He was, without a doubt, sexy as hell. He looked like a Trojan warrior, if that was even possible, and she could not wrap her head around the fact that he looked like that, but she could understand why he spoke the way he did—very overconfident, arrogant, and absolutely gorgeous.

This guy can't be real, she thought.

This chick is gonna be fun. He glanced down at her left hand and did not see a wedding ring. *Oh, and no ring. My lucky day* was all he could think of.

"Could you give me a few minutes to throw some clothes on and dry off?" he asked as he nodded toward another closed door. "I can take you to the office if you would like to have a seat and wait for me there."

"Sure. Please do."

Cory led the way to one of the closed doors, and Belle followed behind. "I wasn't expecting you so soon," Cory commented. "I wouldn't have got a shower right away had I known."

"So soon?" Belle asked with confusion. "We just spoke a little bit ago. I told you I would be over soon. But I can wait a few more minutes so we can get this over with."

"Okay, great. I will be back in a few." Cory walked out of the door.

She could hear a door close just across the hall, where she saw the bunks. *Does he live here? Oh, I hope not. He is a grown man and should not be living here.*

A few minutes later, Cory was back in the office. "Sorry about that. Where should we start?"

About an hour went by, and their meeting was at an end. Neither one was incredibly happy with the outcome, but they knew they had their departments' best interest in mind. He walked her to the front door, and she asked before she walked through, "Do you guys always leave the back door open?"

"Oh, most of the time, yes. A lot of guys forget their keys to the building, so we make it easier. Plus, you never know when some pretty blonde might stumble her way in." He leaned into her when he said that, which sent chills up and down her spine.

Oh my god, what? That was the sexiest thing anyone has ever said to me was all she thought. "Okay, well, thank you for your time, Captain Richards, and have a wonderful day." As she walked around to her car, she became more confused at the reaction she had to him and how comfortable it actually was being around him.

CHAPTER 2

Driving home that evening, she was pretty tired and couldn't wait to see her kids. Winters in Minser were pretty brutal, but lately the weather had been unseasonably warm, so she and the kids took advantage of it. Katie, her babysitter, would meet the kids at home after school, make sure they get their schoolwork done, and start dinner for Belle. This was the new norm since Nate, Belle's husband, passed away.

Cory got home around eight that night; he had some training modules he wanted to get together for the next training night at the department. He was on the committee for that and was a little over-the-top sometimes, but one could never be too comfortable, he always said, because that was when someone would get hurt.

Belle and Cory lived quite different lives and came from quite different upbringings—neither bad, simply different.

After Belle had made sure the kids were bathed, she put them to bed and called her mom to check in and talk about her day. She sat down to relax around ten that night and turned the TV on to watch one of the crime shows she enjoyed watching. As she watched the show, she found herself thinking back on her encounter today with Cory and wondered what his nightly routine was like; what was it like to live in the firehouse?

I can't even imagine. Like how does he go on dates or be with women? Oh, he doesn't. He is not interested in women. Her thoughts were getting the best of her, for sure.

She was something. Was it wrong that I thought of her in a way I shouldn't? She smiled, and I was instantly drawn to her. Not really sure why.

Both of them lay in their beds, their minds wandering back to their encounter and when they would see each other again. They both knew it was a small town, but sometimes paths just didn't cross. However, fate might have had a different plan for them.

* * * *

March 2 was an ordinary day for Belle and Cory at work. That evening would turn out to be a bit different; Mayor Troop wanted to have a meeting to discuss the most recent incidents and to "keep in the loop of the inner workings of the departments." They both knew it was more of a PR tactic for him and his campaign; it was a reelection year for him. The last meeting with him was six years ago, and Belle was not yet hired by Cocala, so she had hoped that what she was bringing to the table was all positive reports and great progress. Cory, on the other hand, was a bit anxious about the meeting since he knew the mayor had heard about the fight that broke out while on a scene and the continued escalation between the two departments.

One positive thought they both had was they'd get to see each other. That put a smile on both their faces. It had been almost two weeks since they first met, and during that time, they both tried to come up with reasons to have to see the other, but to no avail.

"I am ready for this meeting tonight. I think the mayor will be pleased of the progress of the department and how well I have been managing things, not just with Cocala but with Barcher as well." Belle was putting her jacket on as she was telling this to Rose and was getting ready to walk out the door.

"I have no doubt, Mama!" Rose, her daughter, responded; she was such a huge supporter of Belle and this position she was in. Both children, of course, were never really thrilled with the long hours some nights, but they knew it was a part of it, and they respected that. They also became pretty close to most of the guys and gals at the department since their dad passed away.

Leaving for the meeting, Belle leaned in and kissed the kids goodbye and headed to her meeting. Driving up Troop Lane, she became incredibly nervous and panicked. *Oh god, I hope I look okay.*

I have no idea what I am going to say to him when I see him. Wait, is he even going to be there? I am sure he will be. As Belle continued to drive to the township hall, she just kept thinking of his face over and over and how incredibly handsome he was.

"I got it covered, Dad. It will be fine. I know. I know. Yes, I will make him well aware, along with everyone else in the room, that we want Barcher to be seen in a more positive light and will do what we have to do to get that point," Cory explained to his dad as he was headed into the meeting. "You got it, Pop." Cory hung up with his father and headed into the building. Before walking into the meeting room, he sent a quick text to Sara: "Hey, babe! A bunch of the guys are gonna head out for a beer or two at Bud's after the meeting. You don't have to wait up. But if you do, I will make it worth your while :P." He knew that was corny, but she loved that type of stuff, and he knew that when he sent those, she wouldn't get as mad at him if he came home a little later.

Walking into the room were some of Cocala's people already—Matt, their deputy; Jillian, their supervisor; and there she was, Ms. Isabelle Grant. *Lord, she is beautiful. And look at that adorable little outfit she has on. I love a woman who can wear a white tee, tight jeans, and boots. There is nothing sexier, for sure.* Cory had all this running through his mind as he shook everyone's hands and greeted them all. His men had not shown up yet. *Typical for these guys to be fashionably late.* Cory looked around the room as he shook Matt's hand and then proceeded to greet Belle. "Ms. Grant, pleasure to see you once again." As he said that and took her hand so softly, he could feel her shiver just for a second. This, of course, put a half-cocked grin on his face.

She smiled as well. "Mr. Richards, it is nice to see you again as well." As she said that, she wanted to faint with how the butterflies in her belly took over her whole body.

Finally, after a few minutes, the rest of the Barcher guys walked in. "Damn, guys, fashionably late as usual," Cory said with a bit of a ticked-off tone.

"I know, Cap. We are sorry. We were showering and ran out of hot water, so we had to wait a bit for it to come back, and then we still ended up taking a lukewarm shower. One of the probies was washing the engine and used the hot water instead of the cold. We all tried to show him, but you know how probies go 'Nah, I got it. I know how to use a hose and a faucet.' So that's the story," Dom explained.

I swear, they breed monsters over there, Belle thought to herself. *Look at the size of them. Jeez, they are giants compared to most people. It's nuts.* They all had a seat, and Cory took the one directly across the table from her; of course, he did. He looked so sexy and somehow more mature, considering he did not have a towel on for this meeting. *Damn, I wish he had that towel on. Shoot, I wish I were that towel.* She thought all this and did not realize the large smile on her face was visible by everyone in the room. They all looked at her like she was crazy, as she looked at everyone looking at her one by one until she finally got to Cory. He, of course, had to wonder if that smile was a thought about him.

The meeting started about fifteen minutes late, which was par for the course for any township meeting, and the deputy mayor, Laura Holmes (who was one of the meanest people any of them in the room had ever encountered in their lives—actually in most people's lives), started lecturing them about the most recent incident and how that was unacceptable and that if something like that happened again there would be replacements. Everyone understood, and she took a seat. *Oh, yay me, she chooses this seat.* She took the seat closest to Cory—mainly because she had a huge crush on him and was always focusing on him more than anyone else. Cory, of course, took some advantage to that; he would have been foolish not to.

Mayor Troop walked in finally. "My apologies, everyone. I had a small emergency I had to tend too." Which really meant he needed to use the bathroom. Mayor William Troop came from an exceptionally extensive line of mayors for the town, hence Troop Lane (the road Belle lived on), so the family was an old one and just always seemed to be the mayor, someone from the bloodline anyway. He was a nice man; he was short and jolly. And when people looked at him, they were instantly reminded of Santa Claus (which he played the part for every Christmas event for the town). He had a very hearty laugh and extremely deep voice. He truly was an all-around nice man, and most everyone agreed. That was why many were confused by his deputy appointee.

Everyone in the room was given ample time to give their reports and were very thorough with details and stats and such. The mayor seemed incredibly pleased with the progress thus far with both departments and accredited a lot of that to Belle.

"Belle, we are happy with the progress you have been making with the departments and their relationship with each other. That was the huge reason AJ wanted to hire you. I know personally I could not be more pleased with your work so far."

The mayor was genuine in most things he said, and she believed this time was no different. "Thank you, Mayor Troop. I do appreciate those kind words. However, I cannot take full credit for the positive progression of the departments. I believe—and, of course, this is just my opinion—that the leaders now in have played a crucial role in that as well." She nodded to each person in the room, as if to make sure they were recognized as well.

"With that being said, Mayor, I would like to bring up an idea I had that may benefit both departments," Cory piggybacked off the subject from Belle.

Belle had no idea what he was talking about and, in a way, was a bit offended that he had not mentioned anything to her. Not that he needed her permission, but at least maybe if she had known, she could help support it.

"I am thinking we do a group open house. For starters, we have guys and gals"—he looked over at Jillian—"train together. We have a set day each month or however many times we want to do it and have it switch between departments. This way, both departments get the exposure, and the PR looks damn good for all. Not that Ms. Grant is not doing a stand-up job. We need to have some more positive interactions with each other. Ms. Grant and I can work closely on this, if you all like it and, of course, if she is interested."

At this point, Belle was livid and equally turned on at the thought of working so closely with him. *Of course, I am doing an excellent job. Before me, these departments were a mess, and no one wanted them coming to their rescue. I was actually told that before by one of the elderly residents in town.* "Well, I would certainly like to hear more about it. Captain Richards and I can set up a separate meeting next week, and we can go over some details and see what we can get going. How does that sound?" Belle looked around the room, and everyone agreed to that except Cory, and she was unsure why.

"Actually, Ms. Grant, if it's all the same to you, I was hoping we could do a meet and greet this week, Thursday evening around six. We could meet at a neutral location. Say, here. Would that be okay, Mayor?"

Cory was certainly testing the waters with Belle, and it was starting to show. Belle was beyond livid now; she was more insulted than she had been when she first spoke to him. *What an arrogant ass. He really does think he is just God's gift to the fire service. Well, two can play at that game,* she thought. "Actually, Captain Richards, we have a meeting planned already for this Thursday, so like I said, I would appreciate the opportunity for the two of us to meet beforehand and discuss this further. That sound's okay, right?" She didn't give him a lot of leeway to say no.

"Okay, Ms. Grant, it's fine. We can meet next week if that suits your schedule better. I would not want to interfere with anything you have going on," he said with a smile.

"Thank you," Belle replied.

"Great. So it's settled than. Cory and Belle will meet sometime next week, and we can hear all about it when they have figured out the best recourse," proclaimed the mayor.

"Sir, I think someone from this office should be there. Don't you think?" asked Laura.

Cory quickly interjected, "Oh no, Laura, this one will be just an informal meeting with Ms. Grant. We can set something up another time for you to attend," he said with a loving look, a smoldering one. He knew she would fall right into it, and he knew Belle would see right through it. She did, and she did.

"Okay, great. Have a great night, everyone. This fat ole guy is going to bed." The mayor knew who he was and embraced it.

Matt turned to Belle. "Hey, Belle, we are headed to Bud's for a few. Do you wanna come along?"

A SELFLESS LIFE

Belle really knew she should get home but also hadn't been out of the house other than for work or meetings in about two months. "Yes, I would love that. Let me give Katie a quick call and make sure everything is good at home and let her know I won't be too late."

She walked aside to the stairway outside. "Hey, Katie! How are the kids? Okay, good. Would you mind if I went with Matt and Jill to grab a beer at Bud's? I won't be late, you know that."

Katie didn't question Belle at all; she encouraged her to have a nice, relaxing time with them.

"Thanks. I will text when I am on my way home. Tell the kids good night for me."

* * * *

Walking into Bud's was like walking into a bar from the eighties, like that movie with the guy who became the bartender but wasn't any good at first and then turned out to be awesome—yes, that one. Belle walked in last and saw that the guys from Barcher were already there and throwing darts and, of course, carrying on. *One could not lose them in a crowd because they are by far the loudest bunch of guys I have ever met*, she thought and took a seat with Matt and Jillian.

Matt turned to both ladies. "Bottle and tap?"

Both replied, "Bottle."

"You got it." Matt went to the bar to order three beers.

"Jillian, do you ever go by Jill?" Belle asked. *After six years of working here, I never thought of that. Huh, funny.*

"Actually, my parents and family always call me Jelly Bean, and I *hate* it. I am fifty-three years old, and no one should still be referred to by their four-year-old nickname, but dammit to hell, I am. So I would love to go by Jill, but I just can't not hear 'jelly bean' every time someone says it. But if you want to call me Jill, Belle, by all means, feel free. I would not be offended if you did."

Matt came back with the beers, and Belle excused herself to use the ladies' room. As Belle walked to the restroom, you could feel the tension, and not even a chain saw could cut through it. Cory watched her from the other side of the bar. Matt noticed and was on alert after he saw him gawking at her practically.

Getting up from her seat, she could feel him watching her; and in so many ways, she reveled in the thought of it. As she walked across the floor, the sound of her heels clicking on the floor drew more attention than she had planned. She looked up, slowly pushed her hair behind her ear, and saw half of the room watching her. When she saw that he was watching her, she smiled to herself and went ahead to the ladies' room.

Meanwhile, Matt turned to Jillian. "What the hell is he looking at?"

Jillian looked around and realized he was talking about Richards. "Well, I guess he can appreciate an attractive woman."

Bud, the bar owner, was always telling them that he didn't want any trouble. "If you wanna act like fools, take it outside," he would always say. He was tired of having to get new tables, glassware, and sometimes chairs because of the ruckus they would cause.

As Belle came out of the bathroom, she came face-to-face with him, almost walked right into him.

"Oh, I am so sorry, miss. Please, after you." He walked to the side so she could slide past him.

As she did, her arm grazed his; and instantly, she had chills up her spine. *Again with the chills?* she thought. "Thanks." She smiled and turned to walk away.

He lightly grabbed her right arm and seemed to have almost pulled her closer to him. "Can I buy you a drink?" He knew asking was a mistake, but it was one he was willing to make.

"Hmm, probably not a promising idea." She looked up to her friends and nodded as she walked away; she knew if she accepted his offer, it would be a mistake.

The entire bar saw what was happening, and everyone was on the edge of their seats to see what, if anything, was going to happen next.

"Just one? Among friends." He was not taking no for an answer.

She knew it would be damned if she did and damned if she didn't. She looked up into his beautiful, piercing green eyes. "I can't. I'm sorry." And she turned and walked back over to her friends.

CHAPTER 3

That night would be the last time Belle and Cory would see each other for a while. It was a year almost to the day, and the year was nothing short of boring. So much happened in that time, a lot of not so good and a little good. Matt was more involved in their lives since Nate was gone; Belle didn't really mind because it helped JT with coping with his loss. He took JT there every chance he could; JT always said they understand him and love having him around. That was all true; the guys and gals loved having him around. JT was diagnosed with autism when he was six, and it had been a lot of work with him—therapy, social groups, and life skills. He would be turning eighteen soon and would be graduating this school year, something Belle was told might never happen. Having a child with special needs was not for the weak; it built character and patience. It was just a little harder doing it alone now, but luckily, he was getting older, so it was getting a little easier for him to be more independent and do what he liked. Rose was fifteen and was her mom's best friend since they lost Nate.

Belle tried extremely hard to keep with a normal routine every day, and it really seemed to help them all cope with things. Sadly, Nate's death was out of anyone's control, but Belle would lie in bed at night and rewind back to the days when he was alive, trying to recall if there were signs before that she should have seen. The doctor told her that there was nothing anyone could do because when these happened there were no signs, unfortunately. Matt was married to Joan, one of the nicest women she had ever met, and they would both check up on her often. Katie was their daughter, so she was awfully close to the kids and had become even more so with all the babysitting she did. Katie considered Rose ad JT her siblings and truly would do anything for them.

When Joan would come over, she would talk about how the week was for her, check in on Belle, and recently started playing matchmaker. Joan was a nurse and wanted Belle to be happy and not alone. "I just don't want to see you alone. I am not talking marriage. Just maybe get out and grab a cup of coffee at West Tree Café. Could it hurt?"

Belle would look at her and think, *Yes, it hurts like hell. I am not ready for another man in my life.* "I am just not ready, Joan, but I promise when I am, you will be the first to know."

Joan seemed satisfied with that and tried not to push.

About a month and a half after that meeting, there was a call for both fire departments and the ambulance division from the hospital. JT was one of the first responders, and Belle was having a lot of anxiety about it. He was not yet old enough to be considered an adult member, so she always had to depend on the senior members to ensure his safety. She knew how stressful accident calls could be, and to have JT on that scene made her a bit more on edge.

The two companies seemed to have developed a certain respect for each other; many thought it was from an accident they responded to. One late fall day, there was a pretty bad car accident. Mrs. York, whom everyone adored and was a town icon, was driving down Main Street when a drunk driver blew through a red light and slammed into the side of her car, pinning her between the steering wheel and the door. Mrs. York owned the grocery store; she and her late husband opened it many years ago after their son was killed in Vietnam. The store was on Old Sill Road, and she would bring over any close-to-expiration-date foods to Barcher, which was why the crew from there was more focused than ever before and worked expeditiously to get her out of her Cutlass and safe into the ambulance.

Joe was a paramedic on duty and was one of the first to arrive on the scene; he was also Nate's brother. Shortly after, the fire departments arrived, and police were on scene. Cory was the first to get to the car and, at once, went to work on extracting Ms. York. Joe spoke with her the entire time, keeping her calm and focused on him and not on what was going on around her. Joe and Cory communicated together every move the other was doing; and in no time, she was free and, on the stretcher, moved into the ambulance.

When Joe saw that JT was on the scene, he had him perform different tasks for him to help in aiding Mrs. York. Cory was also making sure JT was with the two of them for the duration of the call.

"Mrs. York, we are going to take you to the emergency department to get you all checked out and get a clean bill of health. Sound okay by you?" Joe had a way with words and really knew how to make people feel at ease, which was why being a paramedic was a no-brainer for him. As he closed the ambulance doors, he walked over to Cory and shook his hand. "Great job back there, man, as always."

Cory extended his hand in return. "Thank you, sir. Helmets off to you as well."

As Joe was closing the doors to the ambulance, he could hear JT say "Thanks, Uncle Joe. Be careful." Joe nodded at him and directed him back to the fire truck.

Cory saw this and walked him back to his truck. "Hey, buddy, mind if I walk with you?"

JT looked over at him and continued to walk toward the truck.

After this accident, the tension between the two fire departments seemed to have quieted some—the arguing on scenes, the I'm-the-best mentality was not as clear. It was just...calm. The arguing seemed to have subsided; the rushing to beat each other to the call was minimal. It just did not seem to matter anymore. Some even asked why there was so much tension to begin with. Some blamed Barcher, some blamed Cocala, but very few knew the actual reason. Very soon, though, most everyone would know too.

Unfortunately, not everyone was on the same page.

CHAPTER 4

The chiefs of both departments still had some unresolved issues—Sal Davis, Cocala's chief for seventeen years, and Clay Richards, Barcher's chief of twenty-three years. Sal and Clay were said to be the best of friends growing up in Minser; they were both young firefighters at Barcher when they were old enough to join and loved every second of it. The two had remarkably high hopes and expectations of themselves; most boys did at that age. In the summer of '61, the two boys and some friends were at the local pond, swimming. Clay was up next for the rope swing and was swinging high and pretty fast; all of a sudden, the rope snapped and sent Clay falling onto a pile of rocks into the shallow end.

Sal at once reacted and rushed to Clay's aide. As he came up on him, he yelled to one of the other boys to get help; while the other boy went for help, Sal and two of the other boys went to work. There was some bleeding from his shoulder, and he popped it out of its socket, but he was conscious and making jokes, so Sal knew everything was going to be fine.

The fire department arrived, along with one of the police officers on duty, and they took Clay to the hospital to get wrapped and cleaned up. "Doctor's orders, no firehouse for at least three weeks. This shoulder injury needs to heal." Clay, of course, was not happy with this news; and his dad was even more unhappy. The Richards men had an extensive line of being in a fire department, so there was not a lot of leeway given, especially for an incident like this. Clay had it a bit harder than most of the boys in town. His father was not easy on him and his brothers, and he ran an extremely strict house. Clay spent most of his time at Sal's because he knew he was always safe there; Mr. and Mrs. Davis were the parents everyone turned too and everyone respected in a vastly unique way than the Richards family.

Sal visited Clay every day and helped him with anything he needed. After all, they were like brothers; Sal would do anything for Clay and always knew Clay would do the same in return—at least that was what one would assume.

"Thanks, Sal, for helping me and staying by my side through this. It means a lot to me."

"Don't even mention it. You would do exactly the same for me."

Then Clay was back at it, full force, and something changed in him when he came back to the department. Both were moving up the ranks fast in the department and impressing everyone with the hometown-hero persona, but Clay was taking that a little over the top, some might say.

Things just were that way now, and no one really questioned it. In the blink of an eye, everything changed one day. The town was hit pretty hard by the Vietnam War draft, and Sal and Clay were a part of that group. They were eighteen years old and had no idea what the future held for them. It was 1965, and it truly was an event that not only changed the country as they all knew it but also would change the course of the future for some, good and bad.

Everyone in town was there when the boys were leaving; it was an incredibly sad day for the town of Minser. The war was already well underway, and it was not even a full year yet that it had started, and so many lives were lost, young lives. The fear on the faces of the townsfolk was undeniable and unshakable. Ruth Gibson was one of the local girls who were pretty taken with Clay, but she was a bit younger and knew that an older boy like him would not even notice her.

As the bus was loading, Sal hugged his mom one last time and shook his dad's hand, which ended up in a hug, and walked up the steps and into his seat. He could see out the window at Clay and his family. His brothers all did the typical guy hug, his mom kissed his cheek and squeezed him tight, but his dad was just as hard and didn't break character for his oldest son. He said a few words, but Sal couldn't make them out, and Clay turned and stepped up and took his seat next to Sal. "You good, buddy?"

"Yeah, I'm good."

"What did your dad say?"

"Ah, nothing, just some words of advice."

Clay looked away, and Sal sat there taken aback that he didn't tell him what his dad said. *He always tells me what he says. Hmm, wonder what that's all about.* Sal sat there staring out the window, watching his world go by. As he stared out that window, he had so many emotions and thoughts running through his mind, but he couldn't shake the fact his best friend of fifteen years didn't trust him enough to tell him what his dad said to him. The town watched the bus as it drove out of sight, and at that moment, things were vastly different for Minser, at least for a few years.

CHAPTER 5

"Hey, Belle, how was your weekend?" Jillian asked as she was inventorying the ambulance.

"It was nice, thank you for asking. How was yours?" Belle looked at Jill and waited for a response, but she was so entrenched in her work she didn't hear her. It was seven thirty on Monday, February 21, 2018. Walking into her office, she knew she had a long week ahead of her. *I guess I'm starting with emails so I can get them done and over with for the day.* As she opened her email, she noticed one from the weekend that had no subject—just the sender "cptcr@barcher.com." *Okay. Wonder what this could be about,* she thought to herself as she clicked on it to open the message:

> Ms. Grant,
>
> I hope this email finds you well and that you have a wonderful week ahead. I am not going to beat around the bush. I am a pretty upfront kind of guy, so here goes. Tomorrow is exactly one year ago that we met. Not sure if you remember that or not, but I know I can't get you off my mind and haven't been able to since that day. I don't even know why. It's like I'm drawn to you somehow, like some magical force is pulling me to you. Crazy? Yeah, I know, but I can't help it. I remember that day like it was yesterday. When we got off the phone, I knew I couldn't wait to meet you. And then when I saw you, omg, it was like I knew you my entire life. You were in that gray shirt and pale-blue skirt. I was just

taken aback with just how beautiful you were. Is it crazy to you that we never see each other and we are only four miles away from each other? We have a meeting coming up next week since we never were able to schedule the one from last year, and every other meeting, one of us was not there. I don't know if that's coincidence or not. I just wanted to tell you I am nervous to see you again. And I am sure you are thinking I am nuts, and I just might be. I don't know. I do know that I am hoping that you will be there next week and that this email doesn't freak you out. Who am I kidding? I am sure it does, and I sound super creepy. I assure you that is not my intentions. I just had it on my mind and needed to get it out. I don't expect you to respond to this, and I know you're asking, "Then why send it?" Good question. I hope to talk to you soon.

Cory

What in the hell am I supposed to do with that? While reading this one, he sent a second one, not even ten minutes ago. *Okay, I guess I'm opening this one now too.*

Good morning, Belle,
I am sorry if my email last night was a bit much, and I hope I did not scare you off. I just wanted to see if you could send me over the stats for both of the departments over the past year. I just want to make sure I have all the information correct.

Thanks,
C

Belle just sat there wondering what was happening and what she was supposed to do. *Do I respond to the first one and tell him I feel the same way? Do I just respond to the second one and pretend like I didn't read the first one or that I completely ignored it? I mean, seriously, what?*

"Hey, Belle, you got a minute?" She heard Matt's voice, and she looked up at the door to see him standing there. He looked excited and like something was on his mind.

"Sure, what's up?"

Matt walked in and took a seat. He proceeded to tell her about an idea he had for training and how much money it would cost, and well, she had no idea what else he was saying because her thoughts were on the two emails she just read and how she was going to respond to them.

Once Matt was finished, she went back to her laptop and hit reply.

> Dear Captain Richards,
> I will be attending the meeting next week, and I will be sure to send over the stats for the past year. Thank you for your inquiry.
> Respectfully,
> Isabelle Grant

Thank you for your inquiry? What is that? I put myself out there, and that's the response I get. No way. Not today. He jumped in his truck and sped off to confront her and the response. Pulling into the parking lot, he started to get nervous and then started to have second thoughts about being there. *Well, here goes nothing.* He hopped down from his overly tall truck and walked with a purpose to the front door of Cocala. Cory walked up and pushed the buzzer where the administrative offices were.

Mikey got up to answer. "I got it." He opened the door and was stunned to see who it was when he opened it. "Can I help you?"

"Yes, I hope so. I am here to see Ms. Grant. Could you please tell her that Captain Richards from Barcher is here?"

Mikey nodded and turned away toward her office. He did not invite Cory in just yet. He wasn't really a fan of his, so he figured he could stay out in the cold a little longer. "Hey, Belle? Uh, Captain Richards is here to see you. Should I tell him to go to hell? I would be fine with that if you wanted me too."

"Did he say what he wanted?"

"Uh, nope, just asked for you."

Inside, Belle was a mess, panicking over and over. *Okay, breathe. You got this. He is in your territory. He can't manipulate anything here.* She took a deep breath, fixed herself, and walked out to greet him. She stood there looking around, wondering where he was. She walked down the hall to where the crew was. "Um, Mikey? Where did you send him?"

"Oh, ummm, he's outside still."

She walked hurriedly down the hall toward the door.

"Who is here for Belle?" one of the firefighters asked.

"Richards," Mikey replied.

Everyone in the room looked over at him; it went silent.

"From Barcher?" another one asked.

"Yep," he responded.

Cory stood there while the kid slammed the door in his face, patiently waiting. *Well, that just happened.* It was thirty-four degrees and absolutely freezing, and Cory was starting to lose patience. Standing outside, he couldn't help but remember how unseasonably warm it was this time last year, the day he met her. *Damn, what is taking so long?* He was so cold; he was just turning to walk away when he heard the door open.

"Cory?"

That voice was all he needed, and he was no longer cold. He turned around and was once again completely in awe of her and how naturally beautiful she was.

"I am so sorry you've been waiting out here so long. Please come in."

As they walked back to her office, a wave of weakness came over her; she had no idea what was wrong. She stopped for a second and then continued on.

"Are you okay?" he asked.

She nodded and led him into her office. "Look, let me start with this. I am married. Those things you said, you can't say them. We are professionals, and we have to keep it that way. You understand, right?" The look on her face was desperation and a plea for him to stop. She knew she could feel all those things, but she knew it was wrong.

"I respect that, but I can't help but feel drawn to you. It's like I've known you forever. I said all those things in my email because I needed you to know. I don't know how hard it must be for you since your husband's passing, but I also can't help but be honest with you. I don't know why, and I don't want things to be uncomfortable between us. I just couldn't help it and really needed you to know those things."

Belle stood there behind her desk staring at him, not understanding what was happening inside her. All of a sudden, she felt weak. Her tummy was doing some crazy flips, and she felt more anxious than ever before. Just as she was getting ready to respond to him, a sudden knock at the door was heard. It was Mikey checking on her.

"Everything all right?"

With a smile, Belle responded, "Yes, Mikey, Captain Richards was just leaving."

Cory looked over at her, and his heart dropped when he heard those words. "Yep, I was."

Mikey walked away, and Cory went to walk out the door.

Belle grabbed his hand. "Cory, I am sorry. You have to go. I will see you at the meeting next week." With that, she let go.

He continued to the door; he turned around as she was walking back to her desk. "Ms. Grant, thank you for your time, and I look forward to when we meet again."

With those words, she crumbled and took a deep breath.

This day would be the start of a string of events that no one would see coming—events that would leave things unclear, undetermined, and confusing. A selfless life was the motto they all followed and lived by...the meaning behind this motto just might change the course of history and future as the town of Minser knew it.

CHAPTER 6

Two years had passed since the boys of Minser had been home from war. It was a hard and sad two years for the townspeople, but they managed every day to get through it. Sadly, the town suffered a loss about six months ago. The York family lost their son, Michael, who was only twenty. Mr. and Mrs. York were the nicest people and owned the five-and-dime in town. Their ancestors were part of the founding fathers of the town back in 1894, so they were pretty well rooted in the town and in the county of Trian.

The boys were home on a short leave and knew there was not much time, so they made the most of every minute they had at home. The town planned a dance for the boys and the townspeople so they could enjoy a much-needed break from all the hardships they had been enduring and the sadness they had seen. They all went to visit the York family together and paid their respects to them since they were not home when Michael was brought home. Clay and Sal were excited to stop at the firehouse to see the guys; not much had changed, just a few fresh faces, really. After about an hour or so, the two men left to head home to get ready for the dance at the Rotary Hall. A lot was going through their minds, and none were really prepared for what was about to unveil. The questions were never-ending and really made it hard for them to enjoy themselves, but they made the most of it.

Ruth Gibson was a little older now and was absolutely beautiful. The boys were surprised to see that she was not the same young lady she was when they left two years ago. Clay was the first to notice how much she grew up and matured, and of course, him thinking he was a heartbreaker, he made sure to let her know that he was noticing the change. Ruth brought a friend with her, one of her friends from school who moved here while the boys were at war. Lily Pittner was a naturally beautiful young woman. Her hair was a sunny-yellow blond; she was above average in height, slender, and stunning. Sal took notice of Lily immediately and waited anxiously for Ruth to introduce her to them.

"Ruthie, who is your friend?" Clay asked while walking over to introduce himself. "Hi, I am Clay Richards, and you are?" Clay took her hand and kissed the front of it; she seemed unimpressed.

"Clay, Sal, this is my friend, Lily. She moved here with her family while you boys were away. Lily, this is Clay Richards—whom you have already met, I see—and Sal Davis. Both are great friends of mine and very local."

Lily took her hand from Clay and glanced over to Sal. "Pleasure to meet you both. I am happy you both made it back here to be able to be with us tonight."

Clay and Sal both nodded at once.

"Would you like to dance? It's been a while for me, but I still remember a few steps. Just like riding a bike, right?" Clay reached out his hand to Ruth and swirled her to the dance floor.

It was now just Sal and Lily, awkwardly standing by the punch. "Punch?" Sal asked.

Lily did not know what he was talking about and was a bit taken aback. "I'm sorry?"

"Sorry, I was asking if you would like punch." *Way to mess that up, Sal.*

"Oh, no, that's okay. Thank you, though. Would you like to dance with me?"

Sal, was now taken aback; a woman had never asked him to dance before, let alone one as beautiful as she was. "Uh, yes, that would be great. Unlike my best bud, I don't know how to dance, but I can certainly ride a bike!"

They both grinned at each other and walked onto the dance floor.

As soon as they hit the floor, a slow song came on: "Take Time to Know Her" by Percy Sledge. *Well, isn't this ironic,* both of them thought. Sal went to walk away, but Lily did not give him a chance to. Lily pulled his hand and arm to her and brought her body close to his. Sal's heart was pounding, and he was so nervous, and his hands were sweaty. *This is not the time to start getting all dumb now. Snap out of it, Sal.*

"Are you nervous, Sal?" She looked up at him, and in an instant, he fell madly in love with her.

"I suppose a bit. I have never been a dancer, even though having three older sisters and one younger, you would think I would know what I'm doing. But to be honest, I never paid much attention to that part. I can help you with your hair and makeup though, and they tell me I have great taste in women's fashion. So if you ever need any of that, then I'm your man."

Lily laughed, and Sal was relieved that he didn't sound like a fool to her.

The four friends danced and talked and had a wonderful night. The boys were able to forget about what they had seen and experienced for a while tonight, and it was a nice break for them both. It was 1967, and a lot had changed in their quiet small town, and yet so much still remained the same. One thing the boys both promised each other—well, two things: one was to check in on the Yorks, and the second was not to talk about what was happening over there. It was honestly too hard to explain, and they already met some anti-war groups on their travels to get home. By the end of the dance, they all seemed ready to head home, but they had a fantastic time.

Sal and Clay asked if they could walk the ladies home, and like two teenage girls, Lily and Ruth squealed and happily agreed. It was a beautiful evening. The lights from the mine were bright that night, and they could smell the coal burning (not always the greatest smell, but it kept the town going with the revenue it brought in, plus 60 percent of the men worked there).

They arrived at Lily's house first. "Well, this is my stop," she shyly stated. "Ruthie, do you have a pen handy?"

Ruth's hand went into her purse and handed a pen to her friend.

Lily walked over to Sal. "May I see your hand?" Sal held out his hand; Lily took it and went ahead to write on it with the pen her friend gave to her. "Good night, and thank you for walking me home. I hope to see you tomorrow."

Sal was in shock; he looked at his hand and saw she wrote her phone number on it. Clay seemed pretty ticked off, and Ruth was trying so hard to get his attention. The three walked a little bit further down the road to Ruth's house, where her father was waiting up for her, which was no surprise. She was the only girl of seven brothers, and they were all scary, huge, and didn't have a lot to say.

"So her phone number, huh?" The tone in Clay's voice was quite sarcastic; at least that was what Sal was thinking.

"Yeah, I was pretty surprised."

Clay threw his arm around Sal's neck and pulled it down and messed up his hair with his free hand. "Lucky dog."

Sal knew that Clay had some frustration against him for Lily giving him her phone number, but Sal was pretty happy, and it honestly really brought his self-esteem up a bit.

As the two men walked to their respective homes, they talked about their return date and how they hoped that the guys they left there were, well, still there. As they talked about all this, Sal couldn't help but become slightly depressed, knowing that he just met Lily and in five days he would be heading back to Vietnam. He hated the thought of it, but he promised himself that he would make the most of every minute while he was home. If that meant meeting a young lady, well, so be it. *We could write each other. It would be nice to have someone new to hear from.*

Coming up Main Street, they saw flashing lights ahead and were concerned and curious as to what was happening. The men looked at each other and started to walk faster as they moved closer to the commotion.

When they both realized what was happening, they ran as fast as they could up the incline. "That's my mom's vehicle," Sal exclaimed.

"I know, buddy. I am on it."

"Mom? Mom?"

"Mrs. Davis?"

"Someone tell me where my mom is."

Sal's family had been hit pretty hard with tough time over the past few years. His dad was diagnosed with lung cancer, from working at the mine, and luckily, his mom was relentless and made him go to the doctor after a few weeks of him complaining of not feeling well. With a very intense regimen of chemotherapy, his dad had been in remission for the last year. His mom was the rock that kept his family together. Sal had one younger sister and brother and twin older sisters. The two youngest were still in junior high, and the twins moved to the neighboring town, got married, and had two kids of their own. It was planned.

"Sal, she's over here at the ambulance."

Sal did not know who was talking to him, but he ran over at once to her. "Mom, what happened?"

Mrs. Davis looked up at her handsome son—she always called him that—and held her hand out for his. "Oh, handsome son, I am okay. Just had a deer run out in front of me, and I slammed on the breaks, but I hit his rear end, and he destroyed my front end." She chuckled; he was relieved that she still had her sense of humor.

Clay was explaining to the crew how important the patient was and to drive like their own mom was in the back. Police Chief Troop offered to take Sal in his squad car to the hospital and asked Clay to go to the Davises to let Mr. Davis know and to bring him up to the hospital as well. "Of course, Chief. I am on my way."

Clay pulled up in his T-Bird after running home to grab it and let his parents know what was going on and walked up to the door. Mr. Davis was already waiting for him. "Sir, I was told to come get you and take you to the hospital."

"Is it my wife?" It was like he had an instinct that something was not right.

"Yes, sir. She was in a car accident."

"Okay, well, let's get going, Clay." The men walked to Clay's vehicle. "Thank you, son, for coming to get me and for always being such a great friend to my Sal. He had always looked at you like his brother, and we have always considered you like one of our sons."

Clay smiled and opened his car door.

As they drove to the hospital, which was about a fifteen-minute drive from their side of town, Mr. Davis started telling Clay about how he and the missus met. "Did I ever tell you about the time I met my lovely wife?" Now everyone knew how they met. Their siblings were all friends, but they were the youngest of many siblings. He had five sisters. He had an older brother, but sadly, he passed away when he was only ten. She had four brothers, and she was the first girl born in the Murphy family (since 1901). But they never met until John (Mr. Davis) came home from the Great War, WWI, and he was at a firehouse banquet when "This beautiful angel in white walked—no, no, floated through the door. She was the most beautiful sight I ever laid eyes on, and I saw a lot of beauty when I was out of country."

The way he spoke about Mrs. Davis was one for the storybooks, and it was a goal that so many people wanted to strive for in their own lives. Charlotte Murphy was so well-liked by everyone who met her, and the boys all tried to date her, but if you'd ask her, she had no time for the nonsense. She wanted to go to university and become a nurse. John continued to talk about Charlotte until they arrived at the hospital. "Okay, let's go check on my angel." He exited the car and walked into the emergency room. The Davises were a little older when they started their family because they both wanted to make sure they were financially secure beforehand, so they were a little older than most of the other parents, but they were also well respected and liked by all.

"Hello there, young lady. I am looking for my honey, Charlotte Davis. Could you please tell me where I can find her?"

The nurse smiled and replied, "Of course, Mr. Davis. Follow me. Your son is here also. Is this your other son?" she asked as she glanced at Clay and started for the room.

Mr. Davis nodded and, with a happy tone, responded, "You could say that." He looked over at Clay and smiled. Clay smiled in return, and both entered the room. "Oh, my sweet honey, how are you? What happened?" Mr. Davis sat on the side of the bed beside her and took her hand in his.

"Well, you should see the other guy!" Mrs. Davis was never too serious. She always said, "Life is too short to be so serious. John is serious enough for all of us."

Sal and Clay looked at each other and just shook their heads and snickered softly, while Mr. Davis did not find the humor in that statement. "Charlotte Ann Davis, I do not appreciate the sardonic demeanor you have right now. You could've been hurt much worse than you are." He leaned in and kissed her forehead then her cheek and then finally her hand.

"What's the matter? Does my breath stink?" She laughed when she asked, and Mr. Davis couldn't help but laugh too.

All were laughing now, and the nurse came in to check on them. "Everything okay in here?"

"Oh, we're all okay. Just trying to keep the mood lighthearted," Ms. Davis said, gazing at her sweetheart.

The two young men envied the way Mr. Davis was with Mrs. Davis; it was exactly how a true gentleman was supposed to treat his lady.

CHAPTER 7

Saturday, March 19, was her oldest child's birthday! Belle always made an earnest effort for birthdays in the house. She felt it was most important to remember the day you were born and graced the world with your presence.

Belle heard the car pull into the driveway; it was Joey pulling in with her mom. "Hey, Mom! How was your flight?" Belle was excited to see her. It was over six months since she had seen her last; it was at Rosie's sweet sixteen, and it was too long of a break, she felt. Belle walked into the living room to greet her mom.

"Oh, my beautiful girl! How are you?"

They hugged for what seemed like forever, but that was okay with them. They had a close relationship, and since Belle's mom moved to California, it was hard on them both. Her mom always wanted to live on the West Coast by the clear water, and even though Belle begged and pleaded—and even bribed her at one point—her mom insisted on being there. She always told her she had fond memories of being a young twentysomething there in the '70s and it was an experience like no other and one that everyone should try.

Joe and Rosie walked in behind with grandmom's bags and took them to the back of the house into the guest room. Belle and Nate put an addition about six years ago for her to stay in every time she came to visit. It was quite impressive; she had her own entrance and a beautiful bathroom and a large bedroom.

"Hey, Mom, do you want me to keep this one aside, or can it go back in the room as well?"

"Yes, please leave that here with me. I have something special for my two beauties."

"Mom, you did not have to bring us anything, you know that."

Rosie looked at her mom cockeyed and disagreed with that statement.

"Oh, it's nothing crazy. I was painting again, and I was inspired while I was on my deck." She leaned into the bag and pulled out two packages, one medium and one large one. "Now this one is for my Rosebud."

Rosie blushed every time her grandmom called her that, but she very much enjoyed it. "Thank you, Grandmom!" Rosie hugged her, and she was handed the medium package.

"And this one"—she walked over to Belle with the large package—"is for you, my beauty."

Belle's eyes started to tear up even though she had no idea what it was. "Thank you, Mom."

Rosie was getting impatient. "Mom, can I open it now?"

Belle replied, "Yes, Rosie, go ahead."

Rosie carefully opened the wrapping and revealed a beautiful sea-green-colored glass with the most beautiful seashells and other things found on the beach.

"Do you see what it is exactly?" Her grandmom walked over to Rosie and turned it to the left.

"Oh my, Grandmom, it's so beautiful."

When she turned it to the side, it was made to look like the ocean and the waves crashing into the shore. She was the most talented person the entire family ever knew, and she ran an extraordinarily successful art studio in Half Moon Bay.

"Wow, Mom, that is one of the most beautiful pieces you have ever done for her. Thank you." Belle was always in awe of her mom's talents, and she never ceased to surprise her.

"Okay, Mama, your turn." Rosie was excited now since her mom's was so much bigger than hers.

"Okay, okay." Belle was just as careful as her daughter was when opening the package. As she opened it, she was taken aback by the beauty in this piece of art. "Mom, this is stunning. Is this us?"

"Yes, my beautiful Isabelle. It is when we were on vacation when you were six. We—"

A SELFLESS LIFE

"We went to the Cape that one summer, all of us. I remember. That was one of the best vacations I ever had."

They hugged while tears welled up in both their eyes and slowly fell down their cheeks. Belle smiled at her mom, and at that moment, the days and years after that day that she captured in the painting were just a nightmare in her mind and were insignificant at that moment in time.

Joe walked into the living room at the moment they were letting go of their embrace and wondered what he missed. He looked down at Belle perplexed, and Belle looked up and tilted her head to the side and showed him the painting. He smiled and knew that memory well for her; she had talked about it many times at family gatherings. It was the last great memory she had of her entire family together.

Rosie jumped up. "Uncle, look what Grandmom made me. Isn't it just gorgeous? Can we hang it in my room?"

"Wow, that is gorgeous, Mom. Yes, Rosie, we can hang it. But not right now. We will do it later this evening. We have some things we still need to finish before your brother's party tomorrow. Okay, kiddo?"

Rosie nodded her head and placed her artwork on the coffee table, more so her uncle would not forget that they were hanging it later that day.

While sitting there and thinking back on those days after that day in the painting, she couldn't help but feel guilt, anxiety, disappointment, and too many other adjectives to name about herself. She found her thoughts would often wander to Cory, and she knew it was wrong. She saw what her mom and the rest of the family went through for so long. She did not want to think about him, but there was something that drew her to him. Even though nothing could or would ever happen, the thoughts were still there, and it was hard to rid them from her mind.

"Oh, by the way, where is my grandson?"

"Oh, he's at the firehouse, Mom. You know how it goes."

The firehouse was a positive influence on JT, and Belle was so grateful for the way they had been with him. It was his eighteenth birthday, and he wanted to spend every minute that he could at the firehouse with the "guys"; everyone was considered the "guys" to JT.

"Well, can we take a drive there? I would love to see everyone."

"Mom, we're going to see everyone tomorrow at the party. But we can head down there in a few if you really want to." Belle was finishing cutting some veggies for the tray for tomorrow. "Let me just bag these veggies up, and then I'll be ready to go."

A few minutes later, Belle was ready. "Ready, Mom?"

"Yes, dear. But I was thinking we could walk. It is unseasonably warm for mid-February, and I would like to enjoy it and have some time with my beautiful daughter. Is that okay?"

Belle knew that meant more than what she was saying, and she also knew her mom was relentless and that she should just say okay. "Okay."

The two ladies headed out the door and down the driveway to the sidewalk.

Her mom locked her arm into hers and inhaled while looking at the beauty of the town. "This town has always been so beautiful. Even in winter, the landscape is breathtaking. Don't you think so?"

Belle nodded in agreement and looked around as well.

"So how are you handling everything? It can't be easy on you. I see Joey is around. What does he want?"

Belle inhaled deep and exhaled. "Oh, Mom, I'm not okay. I have no idea what to do. It was like everything was normal a few years ago, and now we are dealing with, I don't even know what yet. I can't sleep at night. I haven't eaten right in months. We still haven't gone through his personals yet. I just can't yet. Mom, I am a mess. I am lost. I am broken. I feel like it is not normal to take this long to move on." Right there on that sidewalk, Belle broke down to her mother.

Her mom held her in her arms so tight and caressed her head with such gentleness it helped to put Belle at ease, at least for the moment. "I cannot pretend to know how you feel or what you are going through. I loved Nate for you from the moment I met him, and I knew he would be such a wonderful husband and father, and I also know that none of this is fair—not for you, for the kids, not anyone. Not for him either. He will never get to experience any of this. You need to celebrate these moments for him and you. I am sure you noticed the number of bags I brought with me this visit, and I hope it is okay, but I was planning to stay a bit longer this time. I know you could use the help."

Belle looked at her mother and started crying again. "But, Mom, you can't leave everything back in California. I will be okay."

"Nonsense. Abigail and Chad will be just fine running everything while I am gone." Abigail and Chad were the stepchildren of Belle's mom from her second marriage, and they adored her (who didn't?).

When her mom moved to California a few years back, Henry (her stepdad) passed away shortly after, and Abigail and Chad were more than willing to head to Cali to help her. At first, Belle thought they were just looking for some money or inheritance; but as it turned out, that was the complete opposite. She was the only mom they knew. She came into their lives when they were ten and thirteen, and she was exactly what they needed in their lives.

As the two walked further, they talked about the events that had been happening over the past six months since she was here last. She asked how Mrs. York was recovering from her accident last year, how things had been in school for the kids, how the firehouse was to her, and how some of the old families were. Belle's mom only lived here for a brief time back in the late '60s. Her dad, Belle's grandfather, was a miner; and he came here for work, like most anyone did back in that time. A few years after they moved here, the mine was starting with layoffs; and unfortunately for her dad, he was one of the first to be let go. So they moved north of Cape Cod, and he found work there. It wasn't ideal, but it was necessary.

Finally, they arrived at Cocala Fire Department. "Did some upgrades, huh?"

Walking into the firehouse, she was at once welcomed by JT. "Grandy!" JT loved her so much and was the only one who was allowed to call her Grandy; it was his own little nickname he made up for her when he was younger and just starting to talk.

"There's my sweet boy." They embraced in a hug, and she began to make a fuss over him. "My, you are too big. What is your mom feeding you? I cannot believe you are eighteen today. Where has the time gone?"

JT was ready to go when they walked in and told his mom so.

"Okay, buddy, we can head home." Belle made him put on his coat. Consistency was very crucial for him, so she made sure to keep up with normal things like wearing a jacket in March even if it was fifty-eight outside. The weather was a recurring thing for Belle over the past few years; it was eerie to her.

CHAPTER 8

"Michigan State University? Lily, why so far? It's so cold and so far from us, your family." Esther Pittner, Lily's mom, was not one to nag; but she was not incredibly pleased with her choice of university, more so because of the location.

"Mama, I told you already. Michigan State University is perfect for me and my career path. I know it's far and cold, but it's honestly not any colder than what we get here. Remember I wanted to originally be on the West Coast, but MSU is offering me a full academic scholarship for art studies, and UCLA offered nothing."

"Oh, I know, but why are they offering you all that money?"

"Because, Mama, they are trying to get more women into their programs and want to offer more to hopefully succeed in getting them to attend. Plus, I am a straight A student, and I have also already taken some college courses for high school students at community college. I am ready, Mama. Plus, what is left here for me? They are doing so many layoffs at the mine. Daddy will be next because he has only been there a little over a year. I am tired of moving. Aren't you?"

Esther looked at her daughter and brushed her hair off to the side of her face. "Yes, my sweet girl, I am. And if you feel that this is the best choice for you, then we will support you, no matter what." She leaned down and kissed her forehead. "Now help me with these potatoes."

* * * * *

"Lilith Annabelle Pittner," the dean of students called each graduate one by one.

Lily and Esther were so excited, and it was the family's most proud moment in history thus far. Once the commencement was finished, Lily ran to find her family. "Oh, Mama, I did it! I am a graduate and soon to be a Spartan!" Lily was the first of her family to graduate from high school and by far the only one attending college. Lily stared off into space for a moment, as if she were already imagining herself there.

"I know, my beautiful girl, and I could not be prouder of you. I will miss you so very much, but we have one last summer together before the rest of your life begins." Esther was beaming with pride, and every parent who walked by them could see it and couldn't help but smile in return.

A few months ago, Lily met what she thought was the man of her dreams, but that did not turn out to be true. She met a coward and boy pretending to be a man. At the dance that night when she met Sal, she was instantly taken by him and was hoping he would reciprocate those feelings; but when she did not hear from him but instead his best friend, she was confused, angry, and hurt. Days after the dance, she received a phone call. "Pittner residence."

"Hi, may I speak with Lily, please?"

Lily's heart jumped, and she was taken over by so many emotions at once. "Speaking!" She did not want to sound too eager; his voice sounded a little different, a bit deeper than she remembered. The next ten minutes were the most crucial and important ten minutes of all of Minser, but no one would know that until many years later. The two agreed to meet at Jackie's Place around 7:00 p.m. the next night.

Lily was so nervous and excited and had butterflies. It was six forty-five the next day, and she was ready to go. The diner was close to her home; it was within walking distance. She said goodbye to the household and headed out for her first of hopefully many dates with him. She was still pretty new to town, but she started to learn her way around town and many of the townspeople. As she walked further down the road, she could see the neon sign Jackie's Place; they really had the best milkshakes and burgers around. Standing outside was this handsome, tall, and well-dressed man waiting for her. He was much more attractive than she had remembered from the dance. She wore her favorite light-green dress with a beautifully hand-knitted cream sweater and her white espadrille heels. Esther pulled her hair up for her, perfectly placed on the crown of her head as usual, with a silky green ribbon wrapped and tied in a bow around it.

"You are the most beautiful woman I have ever seen."

Lily blushed. "Why, thank you."

"Shall we?" he put his arm out for her to take, and they walked into the diner together. And with that, Clay opened the door for his date, and they were led to a booth in the back corner.

As they sat and talked, Lily couldn't help but wonder why Sal had given Clay her phone number. She intended for him to use it; if she wanted to give it to Clay, she would've. It wasn't that she did not find Clay attractive. He was very much so, but she knew how much Ruth liked him, and she never wanted to do anything to hurt their friendship. Lily knew it was not ladylike to press on about why Sal did not call, so she was just to sit and wonder why. Clay was the all-American guy, the one you want to marry and have children with and live in a big house with a really large porch for sitting and a white picket fence. That was the all-American dream, right? Wasn't that what everyone wanted?

The two talked about everything, from the weather to Vietnam. She did not want to pry, so she let him talk at his pace when the subject came up. Hearing about some of the things happening and some things that he saw scared her a little. However, when the firefighting came up, she was intrigued to hear about it. He talked about places he had been and the different history he was learning about while in the war. Lily talked about her future plans and where she came from, why they moved here, and what the future looked like for her family. It was almost nine thirty, and Lily had a 10:00 p.m. curfew. They could not believe time went by so fast. Clay offered to walk her home, and even though she knew it was completely out of his way, she happily agreed.

"Well, here we are," she said shyly.

"Here we are. I had a really fun time tonight. Thank you for obliging me with this date."

Lily leaned up and kissed his cheek, which was quite out of character for her, and ran off. "Thank you again. Call me again."

Clay walked home on a cloud that night; all he could do was replay the entire night in his mind—their conversation, the way she looked and smelled, her laugh, her smile. She was truly the most beautiful woman he had ever seen.

"Hey, Mama, I'm home." Lily leaned in and kissed her mom's forehead and headed up to bed. Esther was almost asleep on her rocker, where she spent most of her nights until Mr. Pittner came home.

Clay's entrance at home was much different. He came home to his dad working on his '58 Chevy Bel Air, which was all the time, drinking his beer and listening to rock music—a little too loud for 10:00 p.m., but no one could tell him that. Clay just walked by him and up to his room. He threw his shirt and shoes into the corner, where most everything landed, and hopped onto his bed. Lying there, one arm under his head and the other laid across his stomach, all he could do was think about her. He was surprised she mentioned nothing about Sal and why he gave him her number. He was relieved about that because it was one thing to lie on the phone, but to do it in person, she might not have believed his story.

The next morning, Lily came down for breakfast and to make coffee for Mama and Daddy; she tried to do that on the weekends to give Mama a break and spoil them just a little bit. She made muffins yesterday, so she put those out and the brewed coffee into the cups, alongside the sugar and cream. "Good morning, Daddy. Morning, Mama!"

"Well, it looks like someone had a great night last night." Her daddy was not too keen on his daughter dating, but he knew it was inevitable.

"Oh, Daddy, you would like him." As she went on about the date, her father looked at her mother and just grinned and let her go on. "He was such a gentleman. But I am still confused as to why Sal would do what he did. We never even had a chance to talk, and he told Clay that he was not interested in getting into a relationship with someone as young as me. I am turning eighteen in three months, and I graduate at the end of the school year. It's not like I am a child or anything." Lily just could not wrap her head around it and still was never sure if Clay was telling the full truth or if he was just protecting his friend.

CHAPTER 9

"Hey, Mom, sorry I'm a little later than expected. Everything going okay here. Guess it's a good thing the party isn't until four, huh?" Belle had some final things she needed to pick up from the supermarket, and of course, without fail, she ran into about four different people, and all wanted to talk and see how she had been. Belle did not have much of a social life. It had been that way since before Nate, so when people saw her out and about, they kept her talking for what seemed to be hours.

"No worries, sweetheart. Everything is going simply fine, and we are coming along perfectly. You didn't miss a thing. Rosebud has been such a major help, and JT is putting up balloons. Well, he's popping more of them than blowing them up for use."

Belle walked in hand in hand with her mom and took a deep breath and walked into her house.

Over the next few hours, they all worked diligently to get this party ready and perfect for JT. Colin, JT's best friend, was the first to arrive; and once he showed up, JT was no help. Shortly after four, many of the guests started to arrive; mostly all firehouse people were invited and a few friends of theirs and JT's from school.

Mikey, who was one of Belle's favorite from the firehouse and really took JT under his wing, walked into the kitchen where she and her mom were. "Hey, Belle, can I help with anything?"

"Oh, Mikey, that would be terrific. Can you take these trays into the dining room and put them where they have their corresponding notes?"

Her mom just chuckled. "Girl, you are the most organized human I have ever met."

So many guests had arrived at this point, and Belle was finally able to walk into the family room to greet them all. People were everywhere in the house. Most of the firehouse guys were downstairs playing on the pool table, taunting one another as to who was better at getting the balls in the pockets, and their childlike humor made everyone laughed when they laughed at that statement.

"Hey, where's Chief at?" Mikey hollered out.

"He is on his way. He was finishing a report before he headed over," Scott hollered back.

As her mom and she were in the kitchen grabbing the candles and small plates, they could hear raised voices, and the roasting began. "Nothing like showing up at the last minute, Chief." "You give fashionably late a whole new meaning." There were so many laughs as the two women walked back.

"Okay, on the count of three," Belle was exclaiming as she was walking with the cake and lit candles.

Her mom followed behind with the plates and forks. "One, two, three."

"Lily?"

She looked up to find where the voice came from, saw him, and knew immediately. "Sal?"

The room went silent; and everyone, especially Belle, was speechless.

Belle stopped like a deer in headlights and just stood there with the candles burning.

"Okay, one more time," Matt said, coming to the rescue. "One, two, three. Happy birthday to you…"

As everyone sang, Belle stared at her mom, and Chief Sal and Lily stared at each other, and the confusion finally set in for Belle. Belle knew truly little about her mom living here; she just knew that she lived here for about two years and then went to college and never came back. She never went into much detail about it or if anything happened, so her knowing Chief was a surprise to everyone.

Once the singing was over, Belle grabbed the cake. "Hey, Mom, could you help me cut the cake in the kitchen, please?"

Lily followed and did not say a word; she already knew what was coming. As the two exited the family room, the murmurs started. "Chief?" Mikey was the first to get started. "Um, how do you know Belle's mom?"

Sal stood there looking around the room, and all eyes were on him. "Well, Mikey, that is a long story—one that I wish not to discuss or have the time to tell." Sal's entire mood changed and felt it was best for him to take his leave. "Matt, please tell Belle I'm sorry but it is best for me to go. Tell her thank you so much for the invite. I left a card for JT on the mantel. Please make sure he gets it."

"Yeah, of course, Chief, but you don't have to go. Stay and have cake. Please."

Sal was very adamant in his departure and shook Matt's hand. "Thank you, but I have caused enough of a scene, and I feel it would be best to go." And with that, Sal headed for the door, grabbed his jacket, and took his leave.

Meanwhile, in the kitchen, Belle was reeling about her mom knowing Chief. "Mom, what is even happening right now? You know what, don't answer that. We will talk about this after everyone leaves. I have so many questions. Ugh, I can't even wrap my head around this right now."

"Yes, sweetheart. I will answer any questions you have. Let's get back to the party."

The ladies walked back out to where the crowd was, and at once, both were scanning the room of guests for Chief/Sal. Lily walked over to the crowd and asked, "Where did Sal go?"

Matt turned around. "Oh, he just left."

Lily couldn't help but become overwhelmed with a wave of the same emotions she had over three decades ago. Lily instantly went for her jacket and walked out the door to see if she could stop him. As she closed the door, she could see that he was just getting to the door of his truck. "Sal, please wait," she called out to him and began jogging to him.

He stood there with his hand on the handle of the driver side door, contemplating to himself as to whether or not to get in the truck or wait to hear what she has to say.

"Sal, please wait. I had no idea you would be here. I had no idea you were even still here. Belle and I don't talk much about the ins and outs of her job. I am so sorry."

Sal looked at her and was reminded of many years ago and that she did not seem to age. "Listen, Lily, there's no need for you to apologize. I had no idea Belle was your daughter. I do not have any control over who the town hires for positions like hers. But thinking on it now, I always knew there was something familiar about her that I could never put my finger on, at least until about thirty minutes ago."

The two stood by his truck in silence, extremely uncomfortable and for too long, it seemed. "Could we maybe talk at some time while I am in town?" She was eager to talk with him because it had been so long, and she had questions that still were unanswered.

He was reluctant to answer. "Sure, that would be fine. I will stop by tomorrow when there aren't so many people. Please tell Belle I am sorry." And with that, he got in his truck and drove away.

Lily once again felt her heartbreak. *Too many times my heart has been broken in this town. This will be the time I heal it*, she thought. Lily walked back to the house; she could see Belle standing on the porch with an incredibly sad demeanor now.

Belle hugged her mom. "Oh, Mom, whatever happened with you and him in the past is very much not over. I have never seen a man that sad to see someone, and I have never seen you so heartbroken. Whatever it is, we will figure it out together."

CHAPTER 10

"Hi, Mama! Yes, everything is going so great here! The snow is a little out of control right now, but it's actually really beautiful." Lily made sure to call her mom every Sunday after dinner to check in and talk about the week they both had. Sadly, a few Sundays ago, while talking, her mom said that her dad was sick; this time, the cancer seemed to come back worse than before (she wasn't sure if that was even possible since it was cancer). She begged her mom to let her come home to help, but her mom refused. She would not let her miss out on this amazing opportunity she had. Mrs. Pittner promised her that if anything were to change, she would contact her at once. Luckily, she had not had to do that; the calls had all been positive ones thus far.

Lily worried every day about her family back home, even more so since the news of her father. She tried to not allow that worry to project from her voice when she spoke to her mom; she knew her mom wanted to hear about the good things. The fun she was having, the new friends she was making—all of it gave her mom a sense of ease knowing she was succeeding in her life. The Pittners moved around a lot on the East Coast. They had to go where the work was, and unfortunately, that meant new schools too often, not many friends, and homes that were not in the greatest condition. When they were in Pittsburgh for three years, Lily was eight, and the home was so dilapidated and looked to be like something that belonged in a horror movie. The people who lived in town stared at the family like they were from another planet, which was not surprising seeing how you could watch over thirty movies on aliens and unidentified objects and creatures during that time; it was easy to see why people thought that about her family.

A SELFLESS LIFE

Lily found comfort in having siblings; it made it a little easier with the constant moving. They always had one another and were all remarkably close; they had no other choice but to be. Their mom always did her best to keep holidays, birthdays, and special occasions as normal as possible. She always made sure that she was at any school event if there was a need, and she was strict on the Pittner children getting good grades in school. Esther knew how hard it was on the children because it was as equally hard for her every time they had to pack up and move. All toll it was nine times in seven years they moved; and they, including Daddy, were all exhausted and ready to settle down and make one of these places home for good.

The Pittners believed that Minser would be that town, but sadly, that was not the case. The family moved shortly after Lily moved away to college, and regrettably, it was outside Pittsburg with a population of less than two thousand people, the smallest town by far. Fortunately, this was the one where they could finally put down some roots and start living the life of a family that was staying put.

"Lily, I wanted to tell you before, but with the news of your father and the move and you trying to get settled in at school, I did not want to cause any more stress for you, but I feel I need to tell you now."

Lily was silent on the other end of the phone; she could not even fathom what her mom was about to tell her. "Okay, Mama, what's going on?"

"Well, sweetheart, a few days before we were moving from the house in Minser, that young boy came to visit, Salvatore Davis."

Lily nearly dropped the phone when her mother said his name; she was in a state of bewilderment and asked her to repeat what she said. "What did he want, Mama?" Lily felt a slight tug in her chest and thought that she couldn't feel this way again; she won't let it happen. Both those men hurt her—one her heart and the other her mind.

"He asked if you were home and if he could take a minute to speak with you. He was so sad, and there was more he was looking for. I explained to him that you went to university in the summer after graduation and I would tell you that he stopped by. He told me not to worry about telling you, just that he was sorry for whatever it was that he did, and he hoped you had much success in everything you were doing."

"Anything else?"

Her mother was silent for a brief minute and inhaled quickly. "Oh yes, that he finished his tour in the war and was home for good now. That was it. I thanked him for stopping by, and we said goodbye. That was the last time I saw him. Even when we were packing the house to move, we did not see him, but that Clay fellow stopped in to help us with boxes and such. What nice young men. I am not sure what happened between the three of you, but it definitely felt like some type of love triangle if you ask me." Her mother laughed aloud and shook her head, knowing that whatever it was broke her daughter's heart and it was something that she seemed to want to keep in the past.

"Thank you, Mama, for telling me, and I am so utterly happy that I will never have to see either one of them again." The conversation continued for a few minutes longer until her time was about to expire. "Okay, Mama, I have to go. My time is about up. I will call you on Sunday. If anything changes with Daddy, please call the dean's office as soon as you can. Promise me?"

Her mother assured her that she would, in fact, do so. "I love you, my sweetheart,"

"Love you, Mama. Give my love and hugs and kisses to Daddy and everyone. Bye." And with that, she retreated to her dorm room.

While she prepped for bed, her thoughts wandered back to a time that she did not want to remember. She thought Clay could've been the one, the man she got to spend every day with, the forever one, but that was not the case. She found out from one of the girls in her class that he was writing to both her and Ruth and professing his love for both girls. Lily was not one for those games in her life and confronted Ruth with the letters from Clay, and word for word, they were the same. Ruth told her she was just jealous and she made those letters up. Now everyone knew that Ruth was head over heels for Clay, and there was nothing anyone could do to change her mind. The last time Lily had any contact with Ruth was absolutely heartbreaking.

"I can't believe you would do that to me, Lily. You know how I feel about Clay." Ruth was irate with her friend.

"Ruthie, I promise I will never speak to him again. I am so sorry for breaking your trust. I never wanted anything to come between our friendship."

Ruth left abruptly and angrily and never spoke to her again.

Unfortunately, Lily was made to look like she was desperate and looking for attention—at least that was what Ruth convinced everyone else about her. The last four months of school was ridiculously hard for Lily, and the few friends she had were no longer because of Ruth's fabricated stories. She received a few new letters during that time and wrote "return to sender" on them until, finally, the letters stopped coming. She never told a soul about any of this, and she had no intentions of doing so. She thought about going to the Davis residence to ask for Sal's mailing address, but she knew that Clay had already gotten into his head and that there was no hope in fighting that. Even though Sal never called, she still had a space in her heart for him; she just didn't understand why it turned out the way it did. She knew she would never find out either and that she was okay with it.

CHAPTER 11

"Joany, I had no idea Mom knew Chief Davis. What...how... I mean, like, I'm at a loss for words." Belle was flabbergasted at this fact and really never knew the timing that her mom and family lived here, but she was starting to think there was a lot more to the story and time line of events and swore she was going to get to the bottom of it. "I thought she lived in Ashland, but it was here. I mean, I know that Ashland is three minutes from here, but I don't know anymore. Has my life been a lie? Oh my god, you don't think Sal is my real dad?"

Joany and Matt looked wide-eyed and at a loss for words at that comment. "Belle, you just need to breathe and wait to talk to your mom. I am sure she has an explanation or story about why and how she knows Chief. And once you find out, I think everything will be fine."

Joany started to put paper plates and trash in the bag and handed a broom to Matt. "Stop being a crazy woman and help clean up this mess from the party since everyone else left us," she said with a smile.

"I am being crazy, but what was that?" Belle was so wrapped up in her mom and the could-be drama, she completely forgot that JT had to take his meds at eight; it was eight forty-five.

"I already took them, Mom." JT refused them.

"I'm sorry, buddy. Grandy kind of has my head all messed up. Thank you for remembering to take them."

Joey was heading out and saying goodbye to everyone. "I'll see ya, kiddo. Belle, if you need anything, you know where I am. I will stop by one day next week when I am on shift and check on you."

Nate's family was from Ashland, and the two met in college. They both attended Pitt; she attended for human resource management and he for nursing. And now some things were starting to make sense; when she told her mom where he was from, she went silent, and her reaction was stunned. But all she said was "Oh, I lived around there. It was only for a short while." She never said, "Oh, I have history there" or "I had a man there"—nothing. Of course, Belle knew her mom moved around a lot in her lifetime before she went to college, and she only spoke of certain things, so this was a huge shock to the system.

After cleaning up from the party, she went in to talk to her mom in the guest bedroom. Sitting down on the bed, she looked at her mom sitting in the rocking chair. "Okay, let me have it." Lily was not one to beat around the bush, but she knew her daughter was.

"Mom, tell me. Tell me when you were here, who was here, how long you were here. I have so many questions I need answers to."

Lily inhaled deep and exhaled slow. "Okay, but not tonight. It is a long story, and you had an even longer day. I want you to be rested and all before I tell you everything. I have never told anyone about my time here, so this will take me some time, and I hope you can understand and just be patient with me."

"Of course, Mom, but can I ask one really important question?"

"Of course, my beautiful daughter."

"Is Sal my real dad?"

Lily gasped. "Oh, sweetheart, absolutely not. Your father was your father. I promise you that."

Belle was relieved on so many levels to know that Sal was not, in fact, her real dad and took solace in that. *However, does that mean Mom knows or knew Chief Richards?* She heard the stories like everyone else, that they were the best of friends until... *Oh my god...it can't be.* Belle said good night to her mom and could not get out of the room quick enough to call Joany.

"Joany, I think my mom is the girl who 'ended' the firehouse and was the reason that a second one was started. Do you remember how we always heard about that girl who destroyed the greatest friendship of all time? I think it's my mom. I think that's why Chief looked at her the way he did. I think it's why she never told me anything about this place. I think she has so many secrets, and I can only hope she tells me what they are."

Joany was hanging on every word she said. "Well, I wouldn't be surprised, Belle. Your mom, even in her late sixties, looks fabulous, and I have seen pictures from when she was younger. She's a total fox."

Belle looked at the phone in disgust. "Ew, don't talk like that, please. I am having a mental breakdown right now, and all you can do is joke, ha ha."

"Oh, I'm sorry. You're right. I shouldn't joke at a time like this." Joany was the forever jokester. "Hey, Belle, guess what?"

Belle was reluctant to answer. "What?"

"Your mom is Lily the Destroyer." She laughed so loud; she couldn't help herself.

Belle even laughed at that comment. "Good night, Joany."

"Night, Belle. Call me tomorrow."

Belle lay in bed that night thinking about everything from the day, from the start to the end; she felt overwhelmed by emotions and was holding back the tears. She knew if she allowed the tears to fall, she would break into a million pieces, and she needed to be strong for everyone right now. That was what was most important. In the darkness, she could see the faint streetlight peeking into the blinds on her window, and she let her thoughts run until she finally fell asleep.

Sunday morning in the Grant house was always focused on family, fun, and food! It was the one day that they were all together. Rosie would get up early and start making Belgian waffles (a tradition Nate started with her many years ago), Belle always slept in, and JT was on his gaming system until it was time to eat. This Sunday was not much different except Lily was there, and there was a lot of unfinished business from the events of the day before. Belle was getting dressed when she heard a knock at her door. "Come in," she said.

"Morning. Okay to come in?" Lily waited for an invite from her daughter.

"Please do."

Lily sat on her bed and patted her hand next to her for Belle to take a seat by her. The mother and daughter sat side by side, something they had not done for many years.

"Mom, you don't have to tell me everything at once. Just tell me about a little bit at a time. We have plenty of time, and I want you to be comfortable telling me at your own pace."

Hearing those words put Lily at ease and knew exactly where she was going to start with her story. "I want to be truly clear on a few things before I start. I do not have any intentions of keeping anything from you, but it will take me some time to get through everything. So much happened back then. I mean, we were kids, but it was such real-life adult experiences. There are some things I'll tell you that I am not necessarily proud of, and there are things you will learn about many of the people in this town—some things you won't like very much, and some things will make you sad. Just know that no matter what, I am still your mom, and I love you very much."

Belle was a little concerned with some of the words her mom was saying and even had second thoughts about all this, but she knew she needed to know. As she sat there looking at her mom, she could see the hesitation and anxiety on her face and didn't want to push her. They could hear the music downstairs and the laughter coming from the kitchen. They smiled at each other, and Lily continued on.

She began, "As you know, we moved around a lot when I was a kid. It was not always easy. In fact, it was really hard. I was lucky enough to have your aunts and uncles, and we kept one another company—the best company, actually. I have been to so many places and have seen so many things, more than most people have in their entire lifetime. I don't regret any of it, except one thing." She stared off into space as if she were going back in time in mind. *It's been almost forty years since I have seen him, any of them for that matter. How do I tell Belle the whole story without her wanting to pack up and leave like I did? What happens if I see Clay—and Ruth? I cannot fathom the idea of how awkward of a conversation that would be. I just need to remind myself that it was a long time ago and I am not the naive young girl that I once was. I am a grown, well-established woman with so many people in my life who love me and would never leave willingly. So here goes nothing.*

CHAPTER 12

Chief Sal Davis walked into his apartment from the supermarket over on Donnelly Avenue and was still dumbfounded and speechless from the previous day's events. *It's been almost four decades since I've seen her last, and yes, she was older, but she was still just as beautiful as the last time I saw her, even more so now. I didn't believe at first it was her. So long ago, she broke my heart, and she left without a word. I know Belle has no idea who I am to her, judging by the reaction she gave. I had no idea who she was either other than a young woman who married the Grant boy, whose dad is a good friend of mine. I never put much thought into who she was before she came here from college with Nate, and I never asked truthfully. The more I think about it, the more I can see the resemblance of the two. Belle looks so much like Lily, it's uncanny. I always told myself that she reminded me of someone and that I always felt as if I had known her already. Jokingly I would say, "Maybe in a past life." I guess I didn't realize how right that statement was until yesterday. What do I do? Do I go back over there and talk to her and demand she tell me why she left and why she chose him? Yes, that's exactly what I am going to do.*

Sal grabbed his coat and hat and started for the door, but something stopped him. He remembered her mother telling her that he needed to let her go and that she needed to be happy without him. So with that, he let go of the doorknob, hung is coat and hat back up, and started to put away the groceries he just bought.

The firehouse was all a chatter, which was not surprising, but this time was a little different. The people of the Cocala Fire Department were all talking about yesterday's encounter with Belle's mom and the chief. "Like, did they date? I mean, did anyone know that Belle's family was from around here?" Scott asked, looking around the room for any clarity from anyone. They all just shook their heads, and none of them had any idea of this. "It was weird, right? Like there was something there at one point. You could totally feel it. But I don't think Belle has a clue. What is the deal with that? She looked just as surprised as the rest of us. I will say, though, her mom is a total babe for being older and all."

"Well, Joey, at least you said older and not old. But I agree. Poor Belle. She seemed so embarrassed and like a deer caught in headlights when he said her mom's name. Honestly, I am pretty shocked that the cake didn't get dropped. I absolutely would've done something like that if my mom had just looked like she had a seen a ghost, only the ghost was alive. Maybe her mom is the one who broke up the friendship between Sal and the tyrant of Barcher. I'm just saying." Jillian was definitely concerned for her friend and was worried about the entire situation.

Later that afternoon, JT walked into the firehouse, and everyone tried to act normal, but it was hard because they were all itching to know what the story was and what was going on over in their house. "Hey, JT! Did you have an enjoyable time at your party yesterday?" Matt asked as he was sweeping the engine bay floors.

"Um, well, I mean, my mom and grandma kind of made it a little dramatic. I really was not okay with that. It was my party, and I didn't feel happy."

Matt just nodded his head and continued on with the cleaning. Sundays at the firehouse were for cleaning and sports. Everyone had a list of light housekeeping to do while they were there, and most of the time, it was not an issue for anyone to clean. Just today was a little different.

"Dispatch to Engine Company 08, Truck Company 91." The dispatcher went on with the call, "108 Spring Glen Drive, fire in the chimney. Fire showing from the chimney. Caller states heavy smoke billowing into the living room. Residents are evacuating now." Everyone at Cocala was racing to get their gear on and get to the fire truck; they were Engine Company 08.

In the Grant home, the scanner radio was always on, and they could hear the dispatch over the scanner. "Copy. Truck 91 en route."

Belle immediately froze when she heard his voice, Cory. She knew instantly it was his voice; she played it over in her mind often. Her heart skipped a beat for a second when she first heard him, and then seconds later, she heard Cocala radio back that they were en route as well. Every time JT was on a fire call, she was a bit nervous, but he knew what to do and how to be safe, and she never wanted him to think that he was not capable, so she never let him know how worried she actually would get.

"Is that Barcher, the 91 guy?" Lily asked.

"Yes, that was Captain Cory Richards." Belle partly said his name on purpose to see how her mom would react to the Richards name, and she did react, but it was more of a frightened look she wore and not an intrigued or disgusted look. "Mom, do you know his dad?"

"Well, who is his dad?"

"Chief Richards, Clay."

Lily had a gut feeling that Belle was going to say that and took a deep breath. "Yes, I do. Sadly, my beautiful daughter, I do."

"Oh, Mom, what did these men do to you?"

Lily took both of Belle's hands into hers. "Oh, Belle, it wasn't them fully. I cannot blame them for it all. I had a role to play in the heartache and heartbreak also. For only living here a short two years, so much happened within that time. I am glad I will be here for a while because I am going to need a lot of time to tell you everything. Just know this one thing: I was so in love with Sal. He made my heart do a crazy little dance the first moment I met him. He was the most handsome boy I had ever seen and was the kindest gentleman you could ask for."

Belle was even more confused now. "But, Mom, if he was all that, why did you not end up with him?"

Lily shook her head. "Clay." That was all she had to say, and Belle knew that it was not going to be a remarkable story—well, it would be, but not the events in the story.

CHAPTER 13

"Babe, I am going out with the guys tonight after our class, so don't wait up." Cory was always trying to find any excuse to hang out with the guys; Sara was so consumed by wedding planning that she never talked about anything but. Cory was not interested in the details of their wedding planning, not because he didn't care or wasn't excited; he just felt he would get in the way, and he wanted her to do whatever she wanted. *Whatever makes her happy, right?* Cory proposed three months ago. The wedding wasn't for another year and a half, but Sara wanted to get started on the plans and details immediately. Sara was a professional photographer; she was well proven in the county and popular among every crowd she came across. They were the picture-perfect couple; and everyone in town, even the county, knew that marriage was just the next step for them.

Cory and Sara were high school sweethearts but had known each other their entire lives. Sara's parents, Mr. and Mrs. Sinclaire, owned the most prestigious law firm in Minser and were upstanding people who were always ready and willing to help the residents of the town. They had two office locations—one was in Minser, and the other was in Ashland. Sara's sister ran the office in Ashland, which was just as successful, if not more so. Minser was a very tight-knit community; when someone was in need or in trouble, the townspeople were quick to come to their aide. The Sinclaires lived a very modest life even though they could live lavishly; they chose to give back to the community and donate most of their earnings to many organizations around the area, one being the children's youth group. When you were a teenager in Minser, you knew that inevitably you would be a volunteer at either one of the fire departments, the CYGM (Children's Youth Group of Minser), or the community library.

Sara was a youth counselor during her teenage years and continued to be a mentor to the upcoming counselors, hosted beginners' photography lessons, and started a clothing collection drive for the adoption center in Ashland, where she also donated much of her services in hosting photo shoots for the children to help increase their chances of adoption. She helped many children over the years, and being around them and getting to know them, she was excited to have children of her own, but she always made a promise to herself that if she, for some reason, were unable to have children, she would adopt without hesitation. Many women envied her, not just because she was with the best-looking man in all the county or because she was "Elizabeth Taylor" beautiful but also because she was genuine, kind, and all-around decent human.

When the businesses owners found out that the two were engaged finally, they all wanted to work with her, from the bakery to the venue, you name it. The engagement itself was perfectly planned out—yes, just like you would see in one of those romantic movies. Cory knew that Sara would expect the pomp and circumstance of the proposal, so the plan was to take her to the lake house and have everyone who needed to be there attend. He had one of her clients set up a photo shoot for her engagement photos at the lake, which was only about a half hour from them; he pretended to overhear her planning it and thought it would be nice for them to get away for a few days before he started his new officers' training with the fire department. She was thrilled at the idea and made all the plans with her client and their getaway weekend.

Cory secretly spoke to her parents, sisters, and brother; her two best friends; the client herself; his parents and brothers; and a few of the guys from the fire department. He hired a florist and one of Sara's employees for the pictures and had an entire crew setting up the most perfect scene under the beautiful willow tree that set back off the lake house property along Lake Arthur. It was one of the most serene and calming settings one could imagine it being; the backdrop was filled with reds, yellows, oranges, and faded greens, thanks to the autumn season waking up.

A SELFLESS LIFE

Saturday morning, they readied for their short road trip. When they arrived, nothing was out of the ordinary. Once they entered the lake house, she intuitively knew something was afoot. As she entered the great room, everyone yelled "Surprise!" Sara was confused but curious as to why everyone was there. Her birthday wasn't until the end of October, so she didn't believe it was for her birthday.

As she pulled away from a hugging embrace with her mom, she was faced with Cory on one knee, holding up a box with the most elegant and tasteful engagement ring one had ever seen. Tears were filling up in her eyes, and her hands were shaking.

He took her hand in his and proceeded to put the ring on her finger. "Sara Marie Sinclaire, you have been the light of my world since we were kids. You have been the one constant in my life, the one I can always depend on to be there whenever I need someone. You are the most genuine woman—person—I have ever had the pleasure of knowing, and I would like the honor of you being my wife. We make sense, we fit, we are right."

There was not a dry eye in the house—well, at least not the women's anyway. The men smiled, and everyone cheered when she responded with a resounding "*Yes!* Of course, I will marry you!"

He stood up and put both hands on her cheeks and kissed her, one of those kisses in the books you'd read about—the one where the girl would feel like she was floating and the guy would plant one on her like he was leaving for war. Yes, that kind of kiss. As they celebrated and carried on, Sara had one question. "Jessica, were we supposed to do a photo shoot for yours and Todd's engagement?" She laughed a little about it as she questioned her.

"No, we are going to do that next month, but I'll call and make an appointment!"

Everyone laughed and continued on with the celebration.

Their parents got along so-so, mainly because Clay enjoyed his alcohol and Ruth thought the Sinclaires acted like they were better than everyone, which was truly not the case. This rift made it slightly difficult for Cory and Sara, but they agreed that no matter what, they loved each other and that was all that mattered. Cory's family was not the easiest to get along with, and he was trying ridiculously hard not to fall into the same category as the rest of the Richards. Sara, on the other hand, was so much like her parents and made it a point to spend as much time with them as possible. Cory enjoyed that since he was treated so well by her family. He walked down by the lake to take in some fresh air. He breathed in, and instantly, his thoughts were taken back some months ago when he met Belle.

Why, on this day, am I thinking about her? I just made this amazing proposal to the woman I love and am going to spend the rest of my life with, but my thoughts turn to her. What? Since the moment we met, I felt a spark—so cliché, I know, but I felt it. I feel like we've known each other our entire lives, different than with Sara. Like something is unknown but known. Cory shook his head as if to shake his thoughts away when he heard the sweetest voice come from behind.

"Penny for your thoughts?" Sara was shyly walking toward him with her hands behind her and a slight grin.

"Oh, I'm okay, sweetheart. I was just looking at how beautiful it is here and how we should come here more often." He felt bad for lying to her, but he knew it was nothing and that those thoughts would fade. Belle had no hold over him, and he wasn't worried.

The night began to end, and most everyone had left. Her parents were the last to leave; everyone helped clean up and said their goodbyes. Mr. and Mrs. Sinclaire congratulated them again and said good night. Cory and Sara stayed to have their own celebration, which was a bit more intimate. It was definitely one of the many things they could do well together without hesitation or much thought. Like he said, they fit.

CHAPTER 14

"Another one bites the dust…" That was what you could hear playing on the jukebox in Jackie's Place. It was a Saturday night in 1980. The place was jam-packed with patrons; and once again, paths were crossing. Sal and Clay had not spoken in years; even if they saw each other out around town, they never said a word—did not even acknowledge the other one. Clay and Ruth were expecting their third child, and they hoped it was a boy this time. Clay prayed for that every night. As they walked in, they were greeted by the hostess. "Hi there, how many?"

Ruth responded, "Two adults, two children, thank you."

"Right this way." The hostess led them to one of the booths in the back; they preferred it there, away from the crowds.

Clay was never the friendliest or most outgoing man in town, but he tried to be cordial to all, except Sal. "What are you getting tonight, girls?" Clay's daughters were four and a half and three and every bit of energetic that little girls that age would be.

Julie answered first, "I'm getting pactakes, Daddy." She was the three-year-old.

"I want a grilled cheese but without cheese," Ginny said with much confidence while playing with the salt and pepper shakers.

Clay and Ruth grinned at each other.

"Sweetie, that's not a grilled cheese then," Ruth started to explain why and made a few other suggestions.

"Okay, Mommy, I'll get a hot dog with fries."

The waiter took their order and hurried off to the next table.

A few minutes later, Ruth noticed Sal walk in and take a seat at the counter. "Clay, Sal is here."

Clay replied, "Okay, so what do you want me to do about that?"

Ruth was on edge often when they went out in public, mainly because she was scared that whatever problems the two men had would eventually manifest into something more. Luckily, to date, nothing had happened, and they just continued to act like the other did not exist. Whenever the two men were in the same vicinity, there was an uncomfortableness and a tension that not even a chain saw could cut. Sal glanced around the diner and saw the Richards family sitting toward the back and thought to himself, *Note to self, do not go back that way for any reason.*

For a split second, Sal's and Clay's eyes met; and just as quickly, they turned away from each other. No one in town really knew what happened with the friendship they had. There were rumors, of course, but no one truly knew except these two men. Neither made a career out of being a firefighter; they both took vastly different career paths when they came home for good from Vietnam. Sal was about to turn thirty in three months, and he landed a job at the tire manufacturing plant in Ashland; and Clay, thirty already, was a foreman for Miller's Construction. Both men worked hard for a living, and it showed on the creases of their faces. At such young ages, they saw more than most did in a lifetime. It was a hard life for them both, but they seemed content in their choices—or at least that was what they wanted the people of Minser to believe. They both stayed active with their respective fire departments, Sal a little more so than Clay due to not having the family aspect in his life.

The Richards family finished their meals and started the process of getting the girls together to pay the check and head home. As they were walking by him seated at the counter, Ruth was eager to say hi. "Hi, Sal. How is everything? It's good to see you. How is your mom?" Clay was stunned and annoyed that she felt the need to speak to him, so he headed off to the register to pay. The silly girls stayed with their mom.

"Mommy, who's him?"

"'Who's he,' Ginny."

"I don't know. I asked you." She was profoundly serious in her response.

Both Sal and Ruth laughed.

"He is one of your daddy's old friends from when they were kids."

Ginny was intrigued, so she hopped up on the stool next to him at the counter. "Really, you knew my daddy back then? What was he like? Was he funny? Did he like pink dresses like me and Mommy do?"

Sal's eyes widened, and he just shrugged his shoulders and looked at Ruth for some help in the situation.

"We can answer those questions when Mr. Davis is not eating his dinner. Let's go, silly girl. Great to see you, Sal. Please tell your mother we were asking for her. Take care." She patted his right shoulder and hurried the girls off out the door to where Clay was standing very pensive and irritated. "Ready?" She took her arm into his and started off to the car around the corner in the lot.

He stopped abruptly. "*Wait*, why were you speaking to him?" Clay never really had any issue with raising his voice in public, especially to Ruth and most especially when she did something he did not favor.

"Clay," she tried to explain, but he just walked away with Julie in tow, leaving Ruth and Ginny to catch up. Clay left Ruth one night at Bud's because she wasn't walking fast enough, and a few of the guys from Cocala walked in and completely ruined his night; he complained the entire night and even the next day when he woke up. Clay was just not a genuinely nice man, and it was a shame that Ruth was so madly in love with him that she couldn't leave him.

Walking into the house, Ruth instructed the girls off to bed and took her shoes off to sit. This pregnancy was a little harder. She believed it was because she was having a boy, but they would know soon enough. Four and a half more months and the baby would be here. Clay grabbed the remote control and turned the TV on. Within minutes of turning it on, a flash came over the news station. "Breaking news," the reporter started. "This just in. John Lennon has been shot. I repeat, John Lennon, singer for the band the Beatles, has been shot and is dead just two months after he celebrated his fortieth birthday." The reporter continued, but Clay and Ruth watched in silence. If there was one band that their generation loved, it was the Beatles.

"I just can't believe it. Who would do that to that poor man? His poor family. Oh, Clay, how terrible is that."

Clay just nodded his head in agreement and was instantly taken back to a time just before he and Ruth got married. Sal watched from the stool at the counter in Jackie's, in shock like everyone else around the world at this sad news. Watching the broadcast, he couldn't help but be instantly taken back to a time when things were a little simpler and a lot less complicated. Both went back in time about eight years when they were home for good from the war and were at a concert neither would forget, for good and bad.

Early August 1972, the guys all wanted to take a trip to New York City and make a weekend of it. Sal was still baffled over Lily leaving and the way she treated him, and Clay was still secretly communicating with her through letters along with Ruth. The guys in his unit called him Casanova Clay, and he enjoyed the attention he got from them and the ladies. Sal was in a different unit, so it was easy for Clay to keep the Lily letters from him. New York City was about a six-and-a-half-hour drive from Minser, but they were excited to take the trip. They needed a break and some real relaxation from the craziness of the world. They didn't have a plan really, just the two of them and three guys from the firehouse. There was still one fire department at this time; it wasn't until 1974 when the start of Cocala was thought up. This was going to be one helluva celebration for them making it home. They knew of too many men who didn't make it home, and they made a promise to themselves that they would live their lives to the very fullest.

The men talked the entire drive, sang, and aired their grievances about the state of the country and the world presently. Sal and Clay talked about the war, not a lot of details but a little about their experiences. No one ever really seemed to want to talk about it, so they didn't get into much detail. Sal mentioned the unfortunate situation with Lily, and Clay made the most fatal mistake that cost them a lifelong friendship.

"You know, I went to see Lily's mom the last time we were home on leave, and she had told me that Lily went off to Michigan to college. I tried to get her mom to tell me why Lily wasn't interested in me and that I did call her the next day but her little sister told me she was out with some local boy. I didn't feel the need to pry anymore and was actually surprised that she was one of those girls. I would've never guessed that in a million years."

Clay looked confused. "What do you mean 'one of those girls'? I got to know her pretty well, and she is not." As soon as the words came out of his mouth, he instantly regretted them and knew what was coming next.

"You know, talking to...wait, what do you mean by you got to know her pretty well? I thought the only time you spoke to her was that night the four of us—me, you, Lily, and Ruth—all went to Jackie's. Am I missing something?"

Clay panicked in his head and wasn't sure how to respond, so he responded honestly, "Well, bud, I ended up getting her number from Ruth. I told Ruth you washed your hand before writing her number down and that you needed it. I had every intention of giving it to you, but I wanted to get a feel for her and who she was before I let my best bud go out with her."

The car went silent. Sal stared at his best friend like he was a stranger; Clay waited for him to respond. Nothing. No response.

CHAPTER 15

"Meeting day, sweetheart!" Lily exclaimed to Belle.

"Ugh, must you remind me? I am all set though. This has been the longest awaited meeting, I swear it. Please stay away from the firehouse, Mom. I don't want any more drama or secrets to occur while I am gone," Belle said, kind of joking but not really.

"Isabelle, would you stop? I promise I will be on my best behavior. Will the Richards boy be there?"

"Mom, he is a grown man, not a boy, and yes, it is just him and me." When the words came out, a shiver went down Belle's spine, and she was quietly excited to see him. She said goodbye to everyone and walked out the side door to the garage, started the car, and exited the driveway down Troop Lane to head to the municipal building for their meeting. All of a sudden, she felt panic and a lump in her throat. *What is this? What are you doing, Belle? Keep it together, girl. It's just a meeting. But I know things now—not a lot, but I know there's history with his family and mine. I don't know exactly what, but I will eventually. Is this why I feel like I've known him my entire life? Why when I saw him, it felt like home?*

Pulling up, she stared at the second floor where the light was already glowing through the window. The blinds were drawn though, so she assumed no one was in there, least of all Cory.

As Belle entered the lobby, she could smell the familiar scent. It was light, musky, and masculine; she knew in an instant it was him. She rounded the corner to the stairs, and there he was. He was on his phone, so he had not seen her yet, but she ogled over his arm muscles and how they tensed. She even caught herself biting her bottom lip and suddenly stopped before he caught her. She walked by him as she ascended the stairs to the second floor. "Captain," she addressed him as she went by.

He was startled by her walking past, almost dropping his phone. "Hey, let me call you after this meeting. Ms. Grant just got here."

When she heard him say her name once again, she got a shiver down her spine.

"Hey there, wait up. We can walk in together." He hurried alongside her.

"You do know it's just you and I right?"

Cory looked at her perplexed. "Wait, Laura told me AJ was going to be here as well. Did she not tell you?"

She was not surprised at all to hear that Laura was the one to tell him and not contact her. "No, I did not know. Oh well, then it will be a fast meeting."

Cory pulled the handle on the door and held it open for her. "After you, milady."

"Thanks."

Walking into the office, they saw AJ was seated at the huge oak table.

"Hey, you two, thanks for being here. I won't take up much of your time, but I wanted to come here in person to tell you some news."

Cory and Belle looked at each other puzzled.

"AJ, what's going on?" The concern in her voice was plain.

"Oh, everything is okay, Belle. I wanted to let you two be the first to know that at the end of June, I will be resigning my seat on council and will be filling in for Mayor Troop. I am sure you both know that he is not well, and he wants to enjoy some of his retirement with Mae."

Cory and Belle were not expecting that, but they both let a sigh of relief out. "Wait, so Laura isn't taking the position?" Cory was a bit surprised about that, and Belle was quite happy.

"Unfortunately, we will be losing Ms. Holmes next month. She received a job offer she couldn't refuse. So she will no longer be with us, but we are finding someone to replace her and my position as well. You think Matt would be interested?"

Belle did not know how to respond. "Oh, I have no idea. I don't think Joany would be very over the moon about that though. She really isn't a fan of politics."

"Well, maybe you can broach the subject with him and her and get a feel for what their thoughts on it?"

"Sure, AJ, I can certainly bring it up."

"Where should we start?" Cory was eager to get the meeting going and had a lot of preparation with him. It made Belle chuckle a bit. "What's so funny?" he asked, grinning.

Belle shook her head. "Nothing. I just didn't expect you to come prepared like this, that's all."

Cory threw his head back dramatically. "Whatever do you mean? There is more to me than just looks and muscle, milady. I am a well-educated man." Such pride he had when he said those words, but he also said them with a smile so as not to seem conceited.

"Of that I have no doubt, Captain."

He loved to hear her say that. "Say that again, please."

"Captain?"

He exhaled and began showing his presentation to her. She took a seat, and he took his. They began to talk about the ideas, feedback, reports, and so much more. Before they knew it, the time was 11:30 p.m.

"Oh jeez, it's eleven thirty. We should really wrap this up and plan a second meeting soon so we can finish this presentation." She held up the notebook to Cory.

"Probably a clever idea," he replied.

They both started to shut everything down and grabbed the paperwork at the same time. At that moment, their hands touched, and both had a shiver run down their spine. They looked at each other, and neither knew what the other was thinking.

I could just kiss him right now. I know how wrong that would be, but I yearn to feel his lips and have him embrace me again but without tears in my eyes this time.

I could just grab her hand and pull her into me and kiss her beautiful lips and feel her skin on mine. I know it would be wrong, but I need to.

He did; he grabbed her hand and pulled her into him, looked down at her, and pulled her chin up to face him.

"We can't do this. We know how wrong it is," she said, breathing heavily.

"I know, but I have never wanted anything more." With that, he leaned down and brought her close to him, and they kissed. The passion was almost illuminating off them. This kiss was one that people would envy for all time. It would be talked about for ages, for this kiss changed the course of the future for both of them. It was left at just this kiss. They knew if they went any longer, this kiss would lead to so much more, and they knew that this was enough. They had already done the damage, and that could not be changed or forgotten.

After the kiss, she leaned onto his chest; she could feel his heart racing. "What do we do now?" she asked.

With a kiss on the top of her forehead, he responded, "I have no idea. I just know I don't regret that, and I have never felt this way before. I feel—and have always felt—like I have known you my whole life. I don't know why or what forces draw me to you, but they do, and I cannot help that. And no, I do not say that to all the girls, in case you were going to say that."

Belle was still in shock that that even happened and didn't want to leave without telling him a few things. "Listen, I know it's late, but I have to tell you something. I have felt the same way since the moment we met in your station and you were in that towel." She grinned. "I couldn't figure out why, what was it that made me think of you, what was it that had me feeling like you were a part of my life for my entire life. It's quick, and I don't have all the details yet, but my mom has some history with your dad and Chief Davis. I have no idea why or how. I just know that they do. Please don't say anything to your father until I have more information. But I did make sure that we weren't related in some way, and rest assured, we are not. But I think this connection stems from them and whatever history they have with one another. Have either of your parents mentioned anything about a Lily or the woman who caused the fire company to become two? Christ, saying that aloud, it's like the Montagues and

Capulets—oh no, does that make us Romeo and Juliet?" She laughed an awkward, uncomfortable laugh.

Once again, he took her into his arms. "Well, if we are, then I guess we will have one helluva love story, huh?"

He kissed her again, she kissed him back, and they knew it was time to go.

Walking down the stairs, she began to wonder when they would see each other again. "Cory?"

That was the first time she addressed him by his first name; he perked up. "Yeah?"

"When will we see each other again?"

"We need to plan another meeting, right? So email me your availability, and let's plan it. But let's not wait too long. I don't want to go another year of not seeing you. I don't think I can manage that." He kissed her hand and left her at her car door.

Driving home, they both were on cloud nine—until they both had a smack of reality hit them when they pulled up to their respective homes. How would they navigate through this? Neither had ever been in this situation, and they were lost but felt at ease in some weird way.

I have to know what Mom knows and her story. Maybe that will help clear things up.

I am not saying anything until I know we are making something of this. If she said "let's go," I'm going. I love Sara, but I have never had this feeling in all the years we have been together.

That night, they both lay in their beds recapping the night, having flashbacks of the kiss. What did Lily know? So many unknowns and questions, but all would be revealed in time.

CHAPTER 16

Belle woke up the next morning absolutely exhausted and terrified about what'd happen now. All night, all she felt was guilt. Most people would not have any sympathy for her, and she knew that. *Cory just got engaged, and they are planning a wedding, and oh my god, what am I going to do? People will find out. What do I say?* That was all about which she could think.

When she got in last night, her mom was already asleep, so she knew she couldn't talk to her about it. Did she even want to though? Would her mom look at her differently because he was engaged? She tossed and turned all night, worrying about what the days ahead would bring.

Belle woke before everyone the next morning and had breakfast and coffee ready. The kids went off to school, and her mom sat with her, waiting for her to tell her what was bothering her. Once the kids left, Belle started spilling the beans, as her stepdad would always say.

"Isabelle, look at me. When I said I would do anything for your happiness because that's how much I love you, I meant anything. Whatever it was or is, I love you, and I need you to be happy before I leave this world. I need to make sure that you're going to be okay and taken care of and watched over. Nate is already gone, so I don't have him to watch over you. I want nothing more for you than to be loved and cared for, but I don't know if Captain Cory Richards is the right guy for that role. Not because I don't like him, but he is a bit wild and engaged to the daughter of one of the most prominent families in the county. I don't think that's going to bode well with them. Plus, there's so much history with me and his father."

"I know. And, Mom, it just happened. I feel sick over it. I don't even know how it happened, but it did, and I can't take back now. I don't even know if he will speak to me again after that. Secretly I am hoping he doesn't so I don't have to face him. Mom, what do I do?"

She got up and went to the door but turned around before leaving. "Isabelle, I love you so very much. I am sorry that you have to go through all this. You did not ask for this so soon in your life together. I have no doubt you will do what is right and handle this situation like you have every other situation thrown your way. If it's going to be Cory, well then, he needs to figure some things out. It's a no-brainer. You're the first choice every damn time."

She walked down the stairs out of her sight, and she cried an ugly cry for so many reasons she couldn't even think of them all. After about twenty minutes, she knew she needed to pull herself together and get the day started.

"Morning, Joan." Belle looked at her mom and whispered, "Give me twenty minutes, okay?"

Lily nodded and went to her room to read some more of one of her romance novels.

"Mom, do you want to have lunch today downtown with me?"

Lily knew what she was up to. "Yes, I would love that. And I can tell you some of the story of myself, Sal, Clay, and Ruth."

Oh wow, even Mrs. Richards was involved in this. This has got to be some story. "Thanks, Mom, I am dying to know."

"I am pretty sure everyone is, Belle."

The two ladies walked down Main Street, did some window shopping, and went into some of the adorable boutiques that were new. Town council wanted to gentrify main street, and everyone agreed it needed some upgrades, but they enjoyed that it still had that old town feel to it. They stopped at Karen's Café for their lunch choice and to talk. They placed their orders and took a seat by the window. It was cold at the beginning of March in Minser, but it was a sunny day, so it made it easy to walk around. The cold did not seem to bother the locals too much, so most everything stayed open all year round.

"Okay, Mom, spill it."

Lily exhaled softly. "Okay, here goes." The next hour, Lily began to retell the history of the short two years she lived in Minser, the first time she met the boys, and how close she and Ruth were at one point. She talked so much, neither one noticed when their food arrived.

Once there was a break in the story, Belle interjected, "Mom, wait, Sal would not do that to you. I have got to know him pretty well, and I am fairly confident when I say that. I just cannot imagine him just dropping you like that. I could, however, see Clay being devious and malicious in his intentions. He's an awful man, Mom. I can't even believe that he was nice at one point."

"Well, that may be the case with Salvatore, but I have not spoken to him since that day. It is pretty crazy that I felt so strongly about someone whom I had only just met. When Clay called and explained how Sal felt, I had no reason not to believe him. He was very convincing. Sal never came around again—well, at least not when he was home on leave. And then I left for college."

"What do you mean? Did something happen? Did he like show up at your school? How romantic!"

Lily shook her head. "No, he did not show up at college, but he showed up at the house before your grandparents were getting ready to move. He stopped by to see me and leave a letter. Your grandmother told me the entire conversation." Lily proceeded to tell her daughter the conversation as well.

"Mom, that sounds more like Chief. He is so genuine, so much like my Nate. He's a good man, and you know, he never married. Oh my god, he never marr—" She stopped midsentence, and all of a sudden, it all made sense. "Because you're the one that got away. Mom, you are the woman who broke up the band, who caused two fire departments to exist. Holy cow, I've heard so much about you but didn't know it was you. Why did you wait so long to tell me?"

Lily gazed out the window. "Well, you see, it wasn't that simple. It was extremely complicated for a long time. You see, Clay wrote to me often, and his letters were scary. They had words in them that raised a lot of concern, so it was necessary to stay in touch with him, if just for him to have someone to write to. I never judged him for any of his letters, but when he came home, he came to see me at school, and it was an extremely uncomfortable visit. Clay was in a very dark place in his mind, and he got a little violent with me one night in my dorm room. He didn't have a chance to actually hurt me because my roommate walked in just as it was getting tense. She saw my face and told him he should leave or she would get security. He left at once, but the rumors that he started about me when he came back here were not pleasant. The words hurt Sal so much and caused such a rift between the two men. Sal swore he would never speak to me again, that I was all but dead to him. That was the last thing he wrote me—actually, it was the only thing he wrote to me. So when I received that letter from him, I knew that there was nothing here worth coming back to, and so I met your father, and we fell in love and got married, and you know that story."

"Mom, I don't even know what to say. I do know that I loathe that man, and now I have even more of a reason to. I don't know how he can have such a wonderful son and be such an asshole." *Oh no. I hope she doesn't notice that comment. I can't explain what happened last night again in one day.*

She didn't seem to notice that Belle made that statement, so she continued on, "When Ruth found out that he came to see and that we were writing to each other during his remaining time in Vietnam, she wrote to me as well. She told me that I was a jealous and terrible friend and that Clay was hers and I needed to move on from him and to stop writing him. That he was not interested in me and that I seemed desperate. It started a little before I went off to college, but it got worse when he came home for good. So I cut off all communications with this town, and I never looked back—well, not until recently anyway."

The two ladies sat and pondered on the words that were just said and ate their sandwiches.

"Mom?"

"Hmm?"

"Have you thought about talking to Sal?"

Lily did not take her eyes off her salad. "I suppose. I just don't know what I would say at this point. It's been a lifetime since I have seen him, and I am still not over seeing him last weekend. But I would like to set the record straight on a few things. I would also like to give Clay and Ruth a piece of my mind, but it's not worth wasting my breathe."

"Well, I can set that up whenever you want to. Or I can give you his address, and you could stop by there. Just throwing that out there. I don't think he would turn you away."

Lily shook her head. "No, dear, I think he would."

"Mom, I saw the way he looked at you at JT's party. He still has something. I can see it."

Lily wondered if her daughter was on to something or if he was in such shock that it only looked like what Belle was describing. "I guess I can. I think we may owe it to each other."

CHAPTER 17

Cory was having a lot of struggles with the night before and what happened. He thought about driving to Sara's studio and telling her what occurred and that he would take whatever she threw at him. Whenever he was having a challenging time with things or needed to vent, he would go to the gym; he knew this was the one place he could let out most of the frustrations he was bottling up. Korn blasted in his ears while he was pushing and pushing his body further and further. The muscle heads were all there this time, his buddies, and all making the most noise in the gym. Most of the time, everyone avoided them to avoid the high testosterone levels spraying off them. The feeling of guilt took over him hard, but it wasn't the part of the kiss and that he had cheated on his fiancée twelve hours ago; it was Belle and Sara and how she was going to handle this all. *Should I talk to her first and see where her head's at? Should I talk to Sara first? No, you definitely will not talk to Sara first.*

"Dude, what's up?" Steve asked. Cory was so enthralled in his workout and music and thoughts that he did not hear him. "Dude!" he said louder this time.

"What?" Cory responded annoyed.

"What's up with you? It's like you're not here but you are."

Cory shook his head and kept pushing himself. Finishing about an hour later, he splashed some cologne on until he could get back to the station to shower. This was his week on duty; a house rule at the station was that one week a month, each officer had to rotate being duty officer. He enjoyed this part of the job the most, because firefighting raced through his veins, and it was the one place he felt home, and now there was Belle to add to that list. Walking out to his truck, he tossed his bag in the bed of the truck (it reeked), hopped in, and drove off to the station. Pulling up to the lot, he noticed a vehicle that he did not recognize. *Huh, wonder who that is.*

Cory walked into the station and heard women's voices coming from the back room. Slowly he walked back toward the room, and he immediately recognized one voice. *Belle? What is she doing here?* He rounded the corner, and there she was—absolutely beautiful. "Ms. Grant?"

Belle and her mother turned around at the sound of her voice. "Hello, Captain Richards. This is my mom. She wanted to come by here and see the old fire station. I hope you don't mind."

Cory was baffled but excited. "Of course, not. Had Steve and Joe been good hosts for you?"

Both Belle and Lily nodded their heads in reassurance.

"Well, if you don't mind, I would like to excuse myself so I can take a shower. I stink pretty bad from the gym." When he said that, Belle smiled and remembered the first time they met and how sexy he was. Reciprocating her smile, he walked out to shower.

"Mom, could you give me a minute? I just want to ask him a question about something from our meeting last night."

Lily looked over at her daughter curiously. "I don't mind. I enjoy hearing these two tell me about their life experiences." She laughed and nodded to the hallway.

Belle walked down the hallway and called out for him, "Cory?"

Cory was alerted to her call and stepped out of the officer's room. "Hey!" He was overjoyed that she sneaked down to meet him. He went toward her, and she stood still, like a statue.

"Cory, listen, this is all so complicated. You and I cannot be. We are professionals, and that's how we need to keep it. I know last night was amazing—well, at least it was for me. But that can't happen again. It just can't. You're engaged to Sara. I have two kids. I am a widow. It's just all too much."

Cory stood there silent and let her speak. When she was finished, he had his rebuttal ready. "I respect that, and I completely understand, but you cannot stand here and tell me you felt nothing last night and not just when we kissed."

"Shh, please don't be so loud," she begged.

"Sorry. It was the embrace. When you cried and I was there and you leaned into me, it was almost as if you became a part of me, like we were joined together at that moment. Please don't tell me you don't feel it, Isabelle. Because if you can tell me that, then I will walk away forever, and we will stay professional."

Belle was silent, trying hard to formulate the words in her mind. "I can't" was all she could muster.

Cory pulled her near and embraced her like he never wanted to let go.

"What do we do now?"

"I guess we need to figure that out, huh?" He swiped her hair behind her ear and put his hands on either cheek and brought her face to his, and they kissed again.

While the two were in their own worlds, they did not notice her mom outside the door. Lily walked back down the hallway a bit and spoke loudly as to not draw attention to herself seeing the kiss and to make sure they had a second to compose themselves. "Thank you, boys! Isabelle, where are you?"

Belle and Cory corrected themselves and put enough space between them so she would not think anything was going on. "Right here, Mom." Belle and Cory knew that was too close for comfort and that they wouldn't be able to keep up this facade for long.

"Oh, there you two are. Are you ready, my dear? It's getting a bit late, and I don't want to accidently cross paths with anyone whom I shouldn't."

"You got it, Mom. Thank you, Captain Richards, for your help. And I will be in touch for our next meeting."

"Okay, I'll wait for your email. Ma'am, it was a pleasure to meet you." He smiled.

"Oh no, sweetheart, the pleasure is all mine," she responded.

Walking to the car, Lily couldn't stay quiet for long. "So do you wanna talk about what it? Belle, what is he going to do about his fiancée? You told me that he just got engaged a few months ago, so what happens? What did he say?"

Belle started the car and drove off toward her home. "I have not been able to talk to him about that yet, but I have thought so many times about me finding someone. It wasn't my plan for that to happen. I don't want to be alone, Mom. It's so hard not having Nate here every day. I know I sound like a silly girl, but I feel safe with Cory. There will be so much attention and controversy over this, I know, but I feel like I am simply lost in a maze. And sometimes I don't know if I want to find my way out, and other times I want to climb my way out. What would you do, Mom?"

Lily gazed out the window as they passed by the old mine, and so many memories came rushing back to her. "Well, I would follow my heart. I wish I did because we would be having a quite different conversation if I had. You have to do what you feel right, sweetheart. I do believe you and he need to have more conversations though, and well, you need to just focus on him and the kids for now. But that's just my opinion."

Everything her mom said was true, and she knew that she was right. That was what she needed to do. But first, she needed to contact Cory so he wouldn't sabotage his relationship and rest of his life. She knew in her heart that the two of them could never be.

CHAPTER 18

The concert in New York City performed by John Lennon was unexpected and one of the only good memories Clay and Sal had from that trip. Little did they know that this would be the last trip they'd every share together and one of the last times they would ever speak to each other. The ride home was long and silent. The other guys tried to get some conversations started, but that unfortunately backfired on them. The subject of jokes came up, so the guys started telling some until Sal had his own joke. "Here's one for you guys. There once were these two guys who were the best of friends until one day one of them was up to his old tricks and thought it would be funny to lie to the girl his buddy was interested in. And then the funniest part was he wrote to her while at war. Pretty funny, huh?" Sal was extremely sarcastic and obviously angry at the entire thing.

"*Oh*, don't get your panties in a bunch, Sal. You're just upset that she continued to write to me and didn't ask for your address once." Clay was not one to be a very sympathetic, caring guy, so what he said was exactly what he meant.

Sal wasn't the aggressive type; he just stayed silent the rest of the drive and swore to himself that he would never speak to him again for as long as he lived. Their buddies knew that Clay was out of line and sided with Sal on this one.

As they pulled onto Troop Lane, passing over the train tracks, Sal just shook his head, knowing what the future was going to be like with him and Clay; and sadly, he knew that Clay had no idea. Clay just went through life bullying everyone, and that made Sal wonder if he had bullied Lily into the friendship or whatever it was they had. He didn't fully believe him. Clay was also a pathological liar, so he wouldn't be surprised if a quarter of what he said was true. He knew the only way he would ever know the truth was if he spoke with her, but alas, that was impossible now. She was gone for good, and so was her family. He would just consider her the one that got away and Clay as the has-been friend.

A few months passed by, and still no contact or communication between Sal and Clay. Clay tried to reach out but never got anywhere with it. He made up lies to Ruth, per usual, and said that Sal was jealous of the fact that Lily would write to him all the time even though he told her not to because they, Clay and Ruth, were together and nothing would come between that. Clay was a world-class bullshitter, and Ruth couldn't see it. Most of the town felt bad for her, but only because Clay really was the meanest man, as mean as his father was. Some didn't blame him for how he was; many others said he needed to grow from what his life was like and try to be a good man. Clay was too far gone, and most think he enjoyed being that way. Ruth was truly blind to it all, at least until one day years later, one encounter changed that.

Lily was driving back to Belle's after dropping JT at the fire station on a Wednesday morning when she spotted Ruth coming out of Karen's Café. She hesitated at first to pull over, but she knew it was long overdue. "Ruth?"

In an instant, Ruth stopped, and part of her was so happy to hear that familiar voice. Ruth did not have many friends since she had chosen Clay over every one of them. Ruth kept walking.

"Ruth, please stop for just a minute."

Ruth stopped. "Hello, Lily."

The women stared at each other for a moment. "I know you just got your coffee there, but do you think we could sit for a minute? There is a lot that I need to say to you. Let me start by saying I am sorry. I am so sorry about everything with Clay."

Ruth put her hand up. "Wait, please, before you continue, I would like to go in and sit. It's pretty cold out here today."

And with that, the women entered the café. Lily placed an order and sat by her old friend. They talked for hours and apologized for how long they were sitting. Karen told them not to worry about that and to take all the time they needed to catch up.

So much was talked about, and a lot was cleared up by both of them. They both knew that Clay was never fully honest with either woman but could never prove it. Ruth knew that Clay would never expect Lily to step foot back in this town, but when her daughter moved here, she knew it was only a matter of time. Ruth explained that she had known who Belle was the moment she met her; she looked just like Lily's mom. She raved about how sweet she was and that she was a great mom to JT and that Nate was a good family man.

"Have you seen Sal?" Ruth knew all this time that Sal was waiting for Lily. He would never tell anyone, least of all her, but she knew it.

"I did. Just last weekend at Belle's home for a birthday party for JT."

Ruth was concerned. "How did that go?"

"Um, as you would expect. He left at once, and I tried to talk to him, but that wasn't the right time and place. I haven't seen him since. Belle said I should see him, but I don't know. It's so crazy how I feel like we never missed any time, you and I. The everyday stranger would see us from afar and assume we were the best of friends."

"We were once, and I have often thought about that friendship, and I often get sad that it was ruined. I am so sorry for how I treated you. I know it was not fair to you. I was so awful back then. I was so bitter. I have been for so long. I have been so unhappy, Lily, but I have no one to talk to. No one cares. Most everyone is afraid of Clay. Can't say I blame them, and I started to become just like him. After his mom passed away, he just became increasingly like his father, and I have tried so hard for my boys to not be like him."

"Speaking of," Lily interrupted, "I met your youngest boy the other day at the station."

Ruth looked perplexed.

"I know you're wondering why I was there. Well, Belle assured me that Clay would not be there, and I really wanted to reminisce a bit at the old station. Cory is just as handsome as can be!"

Ruth smiled. "Thank you. He's been a lot of work. He's always tried to impress his dad and older brothers. The girls he never worried about, but he always felt that he needed to prove himself because he was the youngest and the one who really was interested the most in the fire department. Needless to say, it's been an uphill battle at times with him." Ruth's cell phone rang. "Excuse me a minute. Hello. Yes, I am at Karen's. I will be. Yes. Yes. Okay, I'll see you soon. Sorry about that. It was Clay, of course. I guess I should say goodbye."

Both ladies stood up and went in for a hug. The hug was exactly what they were both missing, and they didn't even realize it.

"Oh, Ruth, thank you for giving me some time to explain some things. I know it doesn't fix everything we've been through, but I am hoping it is at least a step in the right direction?"

Ruth pulled away from Lily. "I don't think you know just how much I needed you today. It was not a great morning for me, and I asked for a sign that I was not, in fact, alone in this world, and you called my name. That's my sign. I'm taking it. Lilith Pittner!" she said with a smile.

They hugged again and exchanged cell numbers and parted ways. Lily watched as Ruth got into her Volvo and drove off down the road. She pointed her face up to the sun and let the warmth of it hit her face. She smiled, her heart was happy, and she was so excited to tell Belle about their conversation.

CHAPTER 19

Belle stepped out onto her back deck for some fresh air; it was a long day at work. She had so much happened at the station, plus everything with her mom, and she still had the unfinished business with Cory that needed to be addressed. Her head was spinning with the reality of knowing that she did not have Nate anymore—her partner in life, her true north—to help navigate through this all. She knew that if he were still here, she would not be in this situation anyway. As she stood there taking it all in, she couldn't help but think about how much had changed in the past few years, and it made her so sad to think about the future ahead without him.

What am I going to do with Cory? I can't imagine what the future would be like in this town for us if we ended up together. My soul hurts. I am sick to my stomach. I just want to cry and make it all go away. I am trying to stay strong for everyone, but it just gets harder every day. I think about Cory too often, and that's not helpful. I still need to talk to him. I have been avoiding him for the past three weeks, and I am running out of excuses to not meet with him again. I emailed him, but I don't believe that was satisfactory enough for him.

Running up Pike Street, Cory crossed over the tracks that led to Troop Lane, where Belle lived. He hesitated for a minute and thought he should turn around. *I should turn back now. I don't really want to risk running into any of them in the house, especially not Belle. She has not spoken to me in weeks. She emailed me with excuse after excuse as to why she can't meet, and I just don't want to deal with the drama.* As he ascended up the hill, he could see their cars in the drive but wasn't backing down now. As he approached closer and closer, he could see there was someone outside but couldn't make out who it was. He got closer and saw Lily going through some boxes.

A SELFLESS LIFE

Lily looked up and saw Cory running, stepped onto the pavement walkway, and stared at him.

Cory was not sure what to do, but he wasn't going to be rude and make himself look guilty, so he waved over to her. "Hello, ma'am. How's it going? What are you doing out here with all these boxes?"

Lily responded, "These are some things of Nate that Belle couldn't bring herself to go through but knew it was finally time. So she asked if I wouldn't mind starting. Figured the kids don't really need to go through it and bring up some sad times, so no sense in keeping it all. Plus, it was before Belle, so it holds no sentimental value to Nate, she said."

"All right, well, don't let me hold you up from your workout." He extended his hand out to shake and bid her farewell. "Thanks. Good seeing you."

Lily held a little tighter in his grip. "Oh, I'm sure we'll be seeing each other more than this."

And with that, Cory continued on his run, and Lily laughed to herself, knowing that Cory would wrack his brain wondering why she just said that to him. Lily hummed a little song and continued on going through the boxes.

As Cory ran away, he couldn't help but wonder what she meant by that last thing she said. *Why would she see me? Shit, does she know? Oh shit, that's not okay if she does. And if she does, how could she stand there looking straight at me? No, she doesn't know. Would Belle tell her? I mean, I guess she could since she is her mom, and those women certainly have some secrets.*

Belle came out front about three minutes later. "Hey, Mom, how ya making out? Need any help?"

Lily waved her over. "Look down the road there a little way."

Belle turned and squinted down the lane. "Okay, what, or should I say who, am I looking at?"

"That, sweetheart, is your future. Ignore the metaphor of him running away and know that when I am not here, he will be running toward this house and your heart." She put her arm around her.

Belle had never heard her so sincere before. Belle held her hand in hers and couldn't help but think of the irony of the conversation she had with herself out back just a little bit ago. She asked for a sign to show her that they would be okay without Nate. Never in a million years would she have imagined that it would be her mom and Cory having an encounter a little while later. "What did you say to him, Mom?"

Lily exhaled. "Let's just say you will most likely get an email from him with a bit of panic in the undertone."

Belle shook her head. "Oh no, why? What did you say?" She always knew her mom was a jokester and expected this to be no different.

"I told him that this wouldn't be the last time we were to see each other. Look, I know it's weird and probably a lot uncomfortable with how okay I am with all this. And trust me when I say I wish it wasn't him, because I don't know if he would understand the caliber of woman he will be getting, but I will say this. I will not have my beautiful daughter at such a young age be alone. JT is going to need a man to show him the ropes at the station, one who knows what they are doing. Rosie is going to need someone to scare the hell out of any boy who comes into her life until the right one comes, and she will need someone to walk her down the aisle. I know you think I've lost it, and I am sure most people would agree. But I know I love you too much to leave this world thinking you won't be loved to the fullest. Isabelle Grant, you are the best thing that has ever happened to me, and I am truly the luckiest person to have had the best parts of you up to now and to call you my daughter."

They stood outside a little longer until Lily could feel her shivering and told her to go ahead in and that she wouldn't be far behind.

"Okay, Mom, I love you. Not much longer, okay? It's cold out, and you're not in any condition to be out here too much longer."

Lily looked at her with a smirk on her face. "Yes, Mom!"

Belle walked into the house and figured it was time to start on dinner. Spaghetti and meatballs were tonight's meal, chosen by JT. She put the pots on and grabbed a glass of sweet tea and sat at the kitchen table to go through some coupons so she could actually go to the supermarket this week sometime. She smiled and laughed audibly at how her mom reacted to Cory passing by and then got a little sad because she knew that she still had yet to talk to him.

The water was at a steady boil, and just as she was getting ready to empty the box of pasta in, she heard a commotion outside. She stopped for a minute to see if she heard it again. She did not, but something in her was telling her something was not right. She went to the bay window in the dining room to see if it was something outside, and in that moment, her entire life flashed before her eyes. She could see her lying there, lifeless. Quickly she ran outside, barefoot, coatless, and terrified. She knelt down and started calling her name. "Mom, wake up. Mom. Mama. Ma." She shook her and yelled for someone to call 911. Immediately she started CPR on her.

One of their neighbors heard her cries and called 911 and hurriedly came outside to help her. "Belle, what can I do? I called 911. How can I help?"

"I can't feel for a pulse because I can't stop compressions. Can you check, please?" Belle said in a shaky voice.

Pete was feeling all over for a pulse, but he had no idea where to feel for it.

"Check under her chin between her throat and neck bone."

Pete was frantically trying to find it, but he was no help with it.

"Where is the ambulance? You told them who it was, right? What is taking so long?" As she continued CPR, she was bumped by another body present. She turned to look, and it was him. Cory heard the sirens and started to run back to his side of town and had to pass by her house again.

"Belle, I'm here. Let me take over. Go in and get shoes and a jacket on. We don't need you catching cold."

Belle dropped back onto the driveway and stared at what was happening; this was a picture she was not ready for yet.

"Belle, go now. I am not leaving her. I promise."

Belle stood up and sprinted into the house and grabbed her snow boots and coat. *I should grab a blanket for him too. He will be cold. Oh, let me get my phone so I can call Dr. Montgomery. Please don't let this be it.* She looked out the window at her mother lying there on the cold pavement and started to sob.

She could hear the sirens blaring up the hill and over the horizon. The entire house emptied, as did Barcher. Katie was not far behind with JT and Rosie. They all feared the scene, and the kids stayed in the car while Katie ran into the house. Belle saw her. "Oh, Katie, I am so sorry. I forgot you were on your way with the kids. Are they here?"

"They are in the car. I told them to stay there until I found out what was going on. Should I go get them?" And with that, Belle collapsed to her knees. Katie knelt down with her and held her close. "I'm here. I'm here." They watched as the paramedics and EMTs came to her aide. Tirelessly they all worked to get this woman, her mother, back to life. She walked outside to be by her mother's side and talk with the kids. It was a moment that was out of a movie.

Belle looked up to the sky, and the sun peeked out from behind the gray March clouds, and she could feel the warmth of the sun on her face and the rays beaming down on her. Cory turned to her in that moment and saw the beauty of the sun glowing around her. Cory knew that was the moment he fell madly in love with her, and he was not giving up on her mother. Paul, Nate's partner at the hospital, stepped in to take over for Cory until a pulse was finally felt. Relief quickly took over the scene, and the sun was covered once again by the gray March clouds. Cory walked over. "Belle, they want to take her to the hospital. Are you ready to go?"

Belle looked at her mom one more time and then looked up at Cory. She agreed. "Why, yes, of course. Cory, do you think you could get the kids inside, please? I don't know how to talk to them right now." Belle laid her hand on her mother's arm and patted it while they made their way to the hospital.

"Yes, ma'am, of course, anything I can do. I'm here." Cory headed off to the car and explained to the kids to come into the house and that he wouldn't let them see anything so they wouldn't be scared to walk past. All the first responders on scene hovered around the ambulance so the kids could not see Lily and the state of the scene.

He walked them into the house, and they were greeted by Katie, and she walked them to the kitchen so the children were far enough away that they wouldn't accidently see anything.

"Hey, guys." Joany was already there waiting for them. She said, trying to clear her throat and hold back more tears, "Come sit for a minute." JT and Rosie sat down, and Joany began to explain to them what happened. The sobbing started from Rosie, and JT got very agitated and started to pace around the kitchen. Joany looked to Cory for help to make sure JT did not leave the kitchen. "JT honey, I know this is too much for you right now, and I am so sorry, sweetheart. What questions do you have?" Joany was so sincere in how she was with him and so patient.

"Is Grandy dead?"

A lump swelled in Cory's throat, and he felt he shouldn't be here for this. This was not his family; he had no right to be here. He quietly let himself out. Joany took the time to explain everything to JT and even to Rosie, and the mood was a little lighter.

CHAPTER 20

As Ruth pulled into her driveway, she could see Clay was home already, and she was going over in her head how she was going to tell him about her lunch and the company she shared it with. It was three thirty, and she was already a half hour getting home due to some traffic issues on the way from Ashland. She got out of the car, went to the back seat for her bags, and headed into the house. She could hear the TV on. He was watching spring season baseball, and he was already fired up and drinking. "Hi, honey," she said as she closed the door.

He turned and looked at her and then at the bags in her hands. "Hi. I see you've been shopping again. Great. What useless crap did you get this time?"

Ruth was already angry, and his tone was not helping. "Just some things for Sara for the wedding and a few little things for the girls since Julie will be by tomorrow with them to visit. Don't forget, okay?" she said as she was walking up the stairs.

He could hardly hear what she was saying and agreed to whatever it was she said. "Yeah, okay."

Ruth was folding laundry that, once again, she asked Clay to do; but she knew he could never be bothered to help her. *Why do I stay with this man? He is just such a mean person. I was so young when I fell in love with him, young and dumb.*

About a half hour passed by, and she could hear a raucous coming from downstairs. Walking to the top of the stairs, she could see Clay rushing around in his office and hollered down, "Everything all right?" There was no response, so she started down the stairs. "Clay, is everything all right?" Clay was busy getting his fire gear together. He had no response; just out the door he went. Ruth stood shocked and confused. *I know he doesn't always tell me the call, but he always tells me that he's leaving. What is going on?* At this point, Ruth started to feel her anxiety creep up, and there was a feeling in the pit of her stomach that she could not pinpoint why. *I'll turn on the scanner. Hopefully I can hear something.*

Ruth knew most of the emergency services lingo and understood certain radio calls. Unfortunately, by the time she got it on, she did not hear where the call was located.

"22-10 to dispatch?"

"22-10 go to dispatch."

A bunch of numbers and streets were said. She heard Troop Lane and had a feeling that something was not right. *What should I do? Is it Isabelle? Lily? No, it wouldn't be Lily.* She only just left her about an hour or so ago and knew Lily was going to pick up the kids from school before heading to the house. *Lily.* It was then that she knew what the feeling was in her stomach. Ruth grabbed her keys and made her way over to the Grants' home, if anything to be with them; there was not much else she could do.

There was no parking anywhere near the house, and there were police officers directing traffic to turn around and head back down toward Cypress Street. She pulled up to one of the officers. He recognized her at once and walked up to her window. "Ma'am, are you looking for Chief Richards?"

Shaking her head, she replied, "No, I am looking for the Grants. I need to be with them."

Officer Novak called over the radio to see if she was allowed to go down to the scene. Paul heard the radio call and asked Joany if it was okay for Mrs. Richards to come down. With her permission, he called back and told him it was okay.

There was so much happening at once. Belle was getting more upset as the minutes went by; Cory was trying to be helpful outside by keeping the scene as respectful as possible for the family. When his father showed up, he went to Cory for the details of what happened. Walking down the pavement, Ruth could see her men standing by the back of the ambulance and rushed over to them. "Cory, what's happening?"

Cory was surprised to see his mom; Clay was even more so.

"Mom, what are you doing here? Is everything okay?"

"Yes, everything is fine. Your father left abruptly, and I turned on the scanner to see what was wrong, and I heard it was Troop Lane and had a feeling it was Lily, and I just had lunch with Lily, and—"

Cory took her hand and brought her inside. He started to explain everything, and Ruth felt a little at ease, knowing that Lily was going to be in the best hands.

A few hours passed, and Belle was leaving the hospital. As she pulled into the driveway with Officer Novak, she could see a few cars there still. Walking up the stairs, she could hear the kids talking and even laughing a little. "Hey, you two, what are we talking about?"

Rosie ran over to hug her mom and sadly cried into her shoulder. "Mom."

Both kids sat on either side of her as she began to tell the kids what happened and why. As she explained, she could see JT getting more agitated, so she tried to keep the details at a minimum. Cory knew but was trying not to draw attention to that fact.

"Is Grandy going to die?"

"Oh, sweetheart." She brushed Rosie's hair behind her ear, away from her face. "No, sweetheart, she is going to be okay. Well, I hope."

"Mom, can I leave now?" JT was ready to go to the firehouse.

"Um, well—"

Before she could finish, Cory interrupted, "I can take you, buddy, if that's okay with your mom."

Belle looked at him in relief. "Yes, that would be fine. I will call when it is time to come home. Love you, buddy."

"Love you too."

She walked over to Cory and thanked him for everything. "I have no idea how to thank you or how to ever repay you for saving my mother's life. I don't know what would have happened had you not been there when you were. I truly am ever so grateful."

"Isabelle, I am sorry to interrupt, but it's the doctor from the ER." Mrs. Richards respectfully entered the room to let her know.

Taking a long deep breath in and out, she composed herself and took the phone.

"Hello, Isabelle, I just wanted to give you an update on your mom."

Belle stood and listened to the news from the doctor. "Thank you, Doc. I will be back over in a bit." Belle hung up the phone and hugged Joany and Mrs. Richards. So she had a heart attack. She is asleep, and he wants her to be that way for a while so they can do some more tests. But it seems she's going to be okay. They want to do an MRI on her brain to make sure there's no permanent damage that they cannot see with the other tests.

CHAPTER 21

"Well, I think I should be heading out too. It is getting late, and I am sure you just want time to be with your family right now. Isabelle, I am so sorry, sweetie. Please call me if you need anything, anything at all." Paul was such a good friend to her and Nate. Not understanding what was going on and how their lunch went, Belle just was happy not be alone. That was one fear she had always had, being alone. Which was a big reason her mom was being so adamant on her finding someone and making her promise that she would or "I'll come back and haunt you both from the afterlife, mwahahahahaha."

The only guests still present were Paul, Joany, Matt, and Sal; it was a weird predicament for both women and even for both men.

"Anyone want to order pizzas? And is it crazy that I am thinking about food after all that happened today?"

Walking over to her side, Paul took her hand and sat down with her on the edge of the couch. "Grief, sadness, crying—all that is different for everyone and hits them differently. Just because this is how you're feeling right now doesn't mean it's going to be that way forever. It'll happen when you're not expecting it. And we will all be here for you, plus a few who have left already."

"Okay, well, let's order pizza."

Paul pulled his cell out of his pocket; he had Apollo's Pizza on speed dial 4. "Uh, what are we thinking?"

"Oh, um, let's do one plain, one pepp, one mushroom and meatball. Oh, oh, and fried pickles. I love me some fried pickles." Belle was twiddling her fingers together, and her side grin was hilarious.

Nodding his head, Paul placed the order. "Okay, thank you. See you in half hour. Okay, well, pizza will be ready in half hour, so I am going to head out and let you all get some time together and eat your dinner. I should've left a while ago. Sorry for overstaying my welcome."

CHAPTER 22

The alarm clock was buzzing at 6:00 a.m., and Belle had hardly slept the night before, which she expected. She made sure the kids were ready for school and dropped them off on the way to the hospital. Day in and day out, she would be by her side at the hospital, helping with her PT and reading her books. Belle was juggling working, taking care of the kids, and visiting her mom at the hospital. It was beginning to wear on her, but it was what needed to be done.

A new meeting was scheduled for the companies to discuss a few things. AJ wanted to have it as soon as possible so the process was finished before the summer. The meeting was set for this Wednesday; it was Monday. Belle immediately picked up the phone to call Joany. "Hey, Joany, do you think Katie would be available to come watch the kids for a bit on Wednesday? AJ called a meeting, and it seems urgent." You could hear a muffled voice on the other end of the phone. "Oh great, thanks! She's doing okay. I have been by to see her every day. They really think she is starting to make progress with her PT. She's not walking yet, but the sitting up in the wheelchair and holding herself up while on stroll seems to be working for her."

The two women continued on in their conversation, Belle talking about her mom and Joany talking about how she stopped in to see her when she could. Joany was an RN in the maternity ward. Belle filled her in about finally going through Nate's belongings. Abigail and Chad were getting all her mom's things to drive them out to her.

"Wow, those kids are driving cross-country. Aw, sweetie, your mom is so loved." Joan really knew that Belle was having a challenging time with this part of the process, but she knew it was necessary. "When do they plan to leave?"

A SELFLESS LIFE

"Chad said they should be ready to head out this Saturday. They have family in some of the states along the way, so they plan to stay with them for their breaks. I am so grateful to them for doing this for her. They were devastated when I called them to tell them. You know they don't really remember much of their mom, so Mom has really filled that role for them since they were so young. I am lucky, that's for sure. And you're right. Mom is loved. Oh, Joany, let me call you later on. Paul and Joey just got here to help with the heavy boxes. Unless you're still stopping over later on?"

Joany confirmed that she would be by around six, and they said their goodbyes and hung up the phone. Belle met the guys outside and showed them where the boxes were to be moved.

Joey saw Nate's old Pitt swag. "Belle? Would it be okay if I took some of this stuff from this box?" He showed Belle the box.

Belle responded with a sweet smile, "Yes, of course. Please look through any of the stuff and see if there's anything you want. I know he would want you too."

As Belle was going through his clothes, she smiled at the thought of how humble he was. He had some high-end clothing but mostly just Walmart or Target things—oh, and the occasional Kohl's attire. He was a simple man; he was extremely modest maintenance and just one of the best one would ever meet.

JT was busy organizing his dad's vinyls, CDs, and cassettes. He had an eclectic music collection; it was definitely impressive.

Things were becoming a little more normal every day. It was still hard without him, but they were actually doing okay. Belle would have a spout of crying every few days, but she was talking with a grief therapist, so that was helping a lot. It also helped her to understand that everyone does, in fact, grieve differently.

Scott and a bunch of the guys from the firehouse were there, moving out some furniture that was not needed anymore. "Belle, this is the most perfect organization you could've picked for the donations. And the Police Relief Association for his vehicle is even more formidable!" Paul was impressed with how Belle was managing all this. "You know we are all here for you, kid, right?"

Belle smiled. "I know, Paul, and I appreciate all this. I really should've done this a long time ago. I guess I just wasn't ready. But with mom coming home in a week or two, I knew I needed to get on it."

The last box was loaded into the truck, and Scott and Eddie volunteered to take it back to the office building so she did not have to. She had yet to hear from anyone at Barcher, but Mrs. Richards stopped by often and brought some homemade muffins, and Belle really wished she would stop because she had gained about ten pounds since. She went to see Lily at the hospital and would talk about wedding planning. Every time Belle heard them talk about that, she would usually have to leave the room for something. It was her way of not having to hear about Cory and Sara, not that she wasn't happy for them; she was just disappointed that she wasted so much of her energy and time on hoping he would be more active in their lives—not as a dad, just as a friend. Occasionally, she would think back to that kiss they shared—well, many kisses—and she would smile that she had some scandalous incident even if only she, he, and Lily knew. It was the most daring thing she had done.

Lily knew how hard it was for her daughter to hear those conversations but also knew that no one else had known about their affair, so she would never lead on about it. Lily had her own secret but knew she couldn't say anything to anyone, and in some way, she was excited about the secret. It seemed to help with her recovery too.

CHAPTER 23

"Good morning, everyone, and thank you all for coming to this meeting. I know it was truly short notice, and I appreciate you all making it a priority to be here," AJ began the meeting. "Let me start by commending you all for a job well done this past year. I know for many of you it has been a rough one." He glanced at Belle. "I wanted to bring you all here today so I could be the one to tell you all that Mayor Troop is retiring. He has some health issues that have to be addressed, and he feels it is best to take steps now to get the right person in the interim of his term."

The crowd seemed surprised, but Cory and Belle knew this already from the last meeting they had with the two of them that AJ was at.

"Oh, AJ, we're sorry to hear this. What can we do?"

The chatter continued, and AJ brought the meeting back to order. "I am sure you're all wondering who will be filling in. Ms. Holmes has left for another position in Pittsburgh, and we wish her good luck. So I have agreed to take the position."

The crowd was pleased with this news. "That's great news, AJ. We need some new ideas in there."

After a bunch of the men and women congratulated him, the meeting continued on. "Okay, so onto my next agenda item—my replacement. This one was a little harder to fill and definitely took some convincing, for sure. This person has lived here for as long as I can remember." He chuckled. "And he has deep roots here, and he doesn't have much experience in politics but is willing to learn." AJ turned around and extended his arm behind him. "Matt, can you come on up and let everyone welcome you as the newest council member!"

The crowd quieted a bit this time; many were more shocked at this news than Mayor Troop retiring. Belle looked over at Cory to see his reaction. He did not seem phased in the least by this; instead, he was the first one to walk over and shake his hand and congratulate him. "Congratulations, Chief!" One by one, people walked up to him and said the same thing and shook his hand.

Belle walked over to him. "*Um*, excuse me, mister, but why didn't I know this?" She gave him a friendly tap on his arm and hugged him.

"Well, I mean, you were the one who convinced me, to be honest." She was confused when he said this to her; he saw her reaction. "Well, if it weren't for you telling me how much help I would get and how good I would be at it, I don't think I would have even considered. Joan is all about it, and I made her promise she wouldn't say a word to you. She didn't, did she?"

Laughing, Belle replied, "No, Matt, your secret was safe with her."

As Belle was saying her goodbyes to the room, she noticed Cory leaving without a word. Hurriedly she walked out the door a few minutes behind him; she was hopeful she would catch him before he left. As she came to the bottom step of the courthouse, she could see his truck backing out of a parking spot in the lot. *Damn, well, there he goes again* was all she thought. She walked to her car and headed to the firehouse since Katie was at the house with the kids; they had an in-service day for teachers at their school.

Driving down Main, she couldn't help but wonder what exactly was going on and why Cory had been acting the way he had to her. She rewound back a few weeks ago and just couldn't understand what exactly went wrong. Part of her resented Sara and the fact that he was still choosing to marry her. Sometimes she wanted to tell her about their short affair—well, kiss—but she knew it wouldn't be fair for anyone and the scandal that it would turn out to be wasn't really worth it for anyone involved. She just resigned herself to the fact that it was never going to be anything again and it wasn't anything to begin with. Pulling into the parking lot of Cocala, her mouth dropped, and she gasped and immediately had butterflies in her belly. *What is he doing here?*

A SELFLESS LIFE

She parked and slowly and cautiously got out of her car. "Captain Richards, is everything okay? Is there anything I can help with?"

He just stared at her—a little creepy at first, she thought—until he finally spoke. "Sara is calling off the wedding."

She stood there in silence, not expecting to hear those words from him. "Um, I'm sorry. Did you want to come in? We can talk about it if you want to."

He shook his head and turned to get back into his truck.

"Wait, you can't come here and lay that on me and then just leave." She walked toward him and pulled his arm to turn him around.

What happened next was so unexpected by Belle, Cory, and the three firefighters standing outside taking a smoke break. Cory looked at her, Belle looked up at him, and he leaned down to kiss all while she was leaning up to kiss him. This was to be the talk of the day among the departments, and the news spread like wildfire. The world seemed to disappear around them once again, but this time was different. There was a new passion behind this kiss, a new magnetic force that everyone who witnessed it could feel.

He pulled back. "I-I-I'm sorry, miss. I had no right to do that. I don't know why I did it again. I am sorry. You do not need to be pulled into my mess. I promise all will be explained when the time is right. I have to go." He hopped up into his truck, and with that, he left.

Belle stood there mad, sad, confused, anxious, and dreading the phone calls she knew she was about to receive. She walked back toward the building and saw the men on their phones; she knew immediately what they were doing. Before she could step one foot in the door, her phone pinged, and she knew it would be Joany. She pulled her phone from her pocket and unlocked it and saw one new text notification:

Joany
Ummm, girl, you need to call me asap.

Belle knew instantly that Joany knew, took a deep breath, brought up her contact info, and hit dial.

CHAPTER 24

"Mrs. Fairchild? You have a visitor."

Lily looked up from her book. "Oh, okay. Well, send them in, please," she said with so much excitement and curiosity. Walking through the doorway to her hospital room was a handsome young man, looking confused and scared. "Cory? I wasn't expecting you today. Everything all right?"

Cory took a seat, a seat that he had been taking for the past week. "Sara called off the wedding." Lily didn't seem as surprised as he had expected. "Why don't you look surprised?"

Lily started, "Cory dear, you are not in love with her. You have been coming to see me every day since the day after I got into this place. And I have not told a soul, but I have listened to every word you said, and I just knew you weren't. You were doing what you thought was the next logical step and what you thought everyone wanted you to do. But, sweet boy, you are not in love with her. You may have at some point, but over time, that does change for some people, and that's okay. What did she say? What did you say?"

"Well, I started with the truth and the fact that I wanted to take some more time to plan the wedding and travel more or whatever we wanted to do. I asked if we had to rush into it, and she got really upset and reminded me of how long we have been together and maybe during that time would have been a better time to bring this all up. She then got really calm and told me I should go to my meeting and that she wouldn't be there when I got home. I asked what she meant by that, and she placed the engagement ring on the counter and walked into the bedroom to pack, I assume." He sat there, tapping his folded fingers against one another, and stared off into space.

"Okay, well, how do you feel now?"

Cory looked at her. "Confused because I ended up at Cocala." He then put his head down because he knew how she would react to that.

"Captain Richards, why on God's green earth would you go there? Of all the places. Why?" She hesitated for a second. "Was Isabelle there?"

Exhaling deeply, he nodded his head yes.

There was a knock at her door. "Yes?" she hollered. It was Joany; panic overcame him. "Hey, Lily! Can I—" As she walked in, she saw Cory sitting down by her. "Oh, I didn't know you had a guest. I'll leave."

Cory stood up quickly. "No need for that. I was just on my way out. Thank you for your time." He walked out the door, and the ladies watched as he went out of sight.

"Um, I had no idea. I guess Belle doesn't know, does she?"

Lily replied, "No, Joan, she does not." She was annoyed that she just disrupted the conversation they were just having. "Can I help you with something, Joan?"

"I told Belle I would check in when I was working, so I wanted to come in and say hi!"

Lily smiled and thanked her for coming by. Her phone rang in the room, and she grabbed it. "Hello!" It was Belle, and her voice was shaking and nervous. "Okay, sweetheart. Come up here and visit with me for a bit. You can tell me everything." Lily had her own suspicions as to what happened between them, but she wanted to talk to her daughter because that was the most important thing to her. She cared for Cory and his situation, but Belle came above anyone.

Lily called for some snacks and drinks so they could talk; it was then that Lily knew it was time for her to tell her the secret she was keeping and hope she would not be upset with her for it. Lily knew it was an extremely challenging time for daughter lately, and the last thing she wanted was for her to think she was conspiring against her or anything to that nature. Belle walked into the room, and her mother was sitting up on her bed, ready to greet her.

"Hi, Mom." So much desperation, it seemed, came from that greeting.

"Hello, dear. I had some snacks and drinks brought up for us. I wanted you to be as comfortable as possible. Come have a seat."

Belle sat down and let out a long exhale and started to eat some of the crackers on the portable table.

"Isabelle."

Belle panicked every time she said her full name; it was either bad, sad, or a mixture of both.

"I want to talk to you about something that has been going on now for a little while, okay?"

Belle just stared at her mom, waiting for her to tell her whatever it was she was keeping.

"After that day in the driveway, I have made a lot of friends here and have had a lot of visitors. Some expected, and some not so much. One visitor in particular was the most unlikely of sorts but one who ended up needing someone to listen and not to pass judgment."

As Lily talked, Belle listened and hung on her every word.

"First, it was just one day, and they dropped off some beautiful flowers for me. I really thought it was a sweet gesture and that would be the end of it. But then it was more frequent and then turned into everyday visits. Some were shorter than others, but they all were nice and well. I think those visits were helpful for us both."

Belle sat there listening; she knew her mom and Sal would eventually start to talk again and that they would find their way back to each other. Belle blurted out, "Oh, Mom." She got up and hugged her. "I am so happy you and Sal are trying again. You don't have to say anymore. I totally approve." The happiness in her voice was unmistakable.

Lily was taken aback and interrupted her, "No, no, my sweet girl, I am not talking about Sal and me. I mean, yes, he has come to visit, but he is not who I am referring to."

Belle pulled away and looked at her, confused. "Well then, who, Mama?"

"Belle, please sit down."

Belle sat back down and allowed her mother to continue.

"Isabelle, what I am about to tell you was not planned at all. The person I am talking about is Captain Richards."

A SELFLESS LIFE

Belle's heart skipped a beat, and it felt like the air was just taken out of the room when her mother said his name. "Mom, what do you mean? He's been coming to see you. What for?"

"Well, that's what I am getting at. He has been fighting these demons inside of him since he proposed to Sara last year, and he knew no one in town would understand and that everyone would say he was foolish and that the two of them were always meant to be. He knew that I had no stake in what the two of them had, and he was right. He confided in me with many things, one of them being you."

Belle snapped her head up and looked straight at her mother. "Me?"

Lily nodded yes. "Isabelle, ever since you walked into his life, that boy has not been the same. These are things he wants to tell you, but he needed to take care of things with Sara and the families first. He came to see you today?"

Belle nodded her head yes. "Yeah, after the meeting. He was just standing in the lot of the fire department, looking out into space. I asked him what was wrong, and he walked away, so I went after him. He turned around and said, 'Sara called of the wedding.' The next thing I knew, we kissed right there in the lot for everyone to see. Oh my god, Mom, I am you all over again except it's with a guy and girl and not two guys."

Lily, perplexed, replied, "What do you mean you are me?"

Belle let out a little laugh. "Mom, you are known as the woman who broke up the firehouse, Lily the Destroyer." She let out the loudest laugh when she said it out loud to her.

"I beg your pardon, Isabelle? I do not find any humor in that at all."

Belle continued to laugh. "I do, Mom. It's funny. Well, it was funny until I just made history repeat itself."

As soon as she said that, the phone in her mom's room rang, and Lily began to talk.

CHAPTER 25

Sitting in his parents' kitchen, Cory couldn't help but feel like he had let them down in more ways than he could count.

"Well, son, I always thought her family was a bit too self-assertive for us anyway. So if that's what you want, then who are we to question it?" Clay was not afraid to speak his opinion on the Sinclairs.

But his mother had a different opinion. "Cory, why are you doing this? I thought this was what you wanted. I thought you were in love with Sara. What happened? Did she meet someone else? Did you?"

Cory felt so ashamed; he almost just wanted to run away from all this. He did this; he knew it. He was the cause of all this, and he didn't know how to fix it. "I'm sorry, Mom. It's how I feel. I want to be happy, and for the past year, I have more clarity now than I ever have in my entire life. You asked if she met someone. No, she did not. She has always been faithful."

Now both were looking at him, waiting for the other question to be answered. "Well, did you, son?" His father was never concerned about his personal affair but was genuinely concerned this time.

Cory stared down at his hands and the kitchen table and then at his parents. "Yes, I have."

They both gasped and went silent.

"I'm sorry for disappointing you." With that, he excused himself and left.

Ruth and Clay just shook their heads in disbelief. "Who? How? When could he have possibly met someone else, Clay? He goes nowhere except work and the apartment, occasionally Bud's, the gym, and…"

Clay looked over at Ruth. "Ruthie, why did you stop? What is it?"

Ruth got up and walked over to the phone, dialed it, and sat back down. "Yes, room 3021, please."

Clay knew what was happening now. "Oh."

"Hey, Lily, how are you doing? Oh, she is, is she? How is she doing? Oh, that's so good to hear. I was hoping we could talk about something. Could you give me a call back after Belle is done visiting?" Ruth nodded her head as if Lily could see her. "Okay, yes, great! Yep, we will talk soon." Ruth hung up the phone and looked at her husband. "It's Belle. I just know it."

Clay was astounded that she said that; never would he thought he would hear that from her. "Why do you think that?"

Ruth glared at her husband. "Call it mother's intuition."

Clay was overcome with a mix of emotions and memories of days gone by. *I hope that is not the case and she is wrong. I don't know about having this back in my life again. Her mother broke my heart, but Ruth can never know that. Shit, what am I going to do if it is?* "Ruth, what if it is? What do we do? I don't have a problem with that girl, and I feel bad that she lost her husband, but it's not right. He doesn't even know her."

Ruth continued to prep dinner for tonight's visit to Lily. Every Wednesday, she went to see her with dinner and catch up on the weekend and all. Tonight's visit was going to be a little more interesting and hopefully not negative. "I just want some answers, and we know our son certainly isn't going to give us any." Chopping the carrots, all she could do was think about what he said and that it was most likely Belle. She didn't have a problem with her either, but she wanted more for Cory. She wanted him to have his own family, and with Belle, it was a family that he didn't create.

Clay left for the firehouse to get some paperwork done and to spend some time alone to think about what was happening. Pulling into the lot, he saw Cory's truck and thought it would be a perfect opportunity to talk with him.

"Hey, Chief! How's it going?" one of the staff asked.

"Fine, thanks. Have you seen my son?"

Kevin answered from on top of the truck, "He's back in his office, Chief."

Clay nodded and headed for the back office. As he was walking down the hall, he could hear voices coming from the office. Upon entering the door, he saw his son sitting behind the desk and Jason, his best friend, standing on the other side. "Hey, guys, what's going on?"

Cory and Jason greeted him, and they ended their conversation.

"Oh, nothing, Pop. Jason was just heading back out."

"Oh, you don't have to leave on my account." Clay patted Jason on the shoulder and took a seat.

"Eh, I got a lot of work to finish, Chief. Cory, I'll talk to you later on." Jason left, and now it was just the two of them, and you could cut the tension with a chain saw.

"What's up, Pop?"

Clay shook his head "Son, I'm going to ask you this one time and one time only, okay?"

Cory nodded his head. "Okay."

"Is the other woman Isabelle Grant?"

Holy shit, how did he know? The panic was written all over his face.

"I knew it. You don't even have to answer" Clay got up and walked out of the office. Cory was stunned and didn't know how to react. He just sat there, thinking more and more.

Clay walked into his office and closed the door behind, shaking his head and wondering what he was thinking. *Maybe he doesn't know who her mother is to me, what our past is. Should I tell him?* Before he could pick up the phone receiver, Cory was already knocking on his door.

"Dad, all right if I come in?"

Clay looked up and pointed to the chair. "Yeah, of course, son."

The Richards men never had a close relationship with one another, so the way Clay was acting was very out of character, and Cory was really taken aback by it. "Can I just say a few things?" Cory was starting to explain to his dad everything that took place over the past year, but Clay had to interrupt him.

"Cory, before you do, I need to tell you a few things about my past. I know Lily, Belle's mom, from many years ago when she and her family lived here for a brief time. We—"

Before he could continue, Cory interjected, "Dad, I know all this already. Lily told Belle everything, and we know that you two talked but it got all mixed up because of mom, Chief Davis, and you."

Clay was shocked that he said all this. "Me? I didn't do anything to that woman. She broke my heart." He got louder with each word.

Cory sat there confused. "What do you mean she broke your heart? Dad, is that even possible? I mean, no offense, but you're not the easiest man to talk to."

Clay continued, "That may be, but yes, she broke my heart. I know everyone thinks it was all my doing, but I was ready to come home to ask her to marry me. I wrote to your mom while in Nam, but I did that as friends. She and I had known each other her entire life, and she was having some challenging times back home, so she wrote me, and I wrote her as a friend. I wrote Lily too, and one day, out of the blue, she sent me this letter telling me that I was an awful man and that to take advantage of two women's emotions was simply wrong and that she never wanted to speak to me again and didn't care if she saw me again. Devastated, I tell ya, that's what I was, utterly devastated." Clay was visibly upset talking about this, something Cory had never seen before.

"Dad, I didn't know any of this. Why didn't you write her and explain everything?"

Clay hemmed and hawed. "Your mother. She had got to Lily. She told her things that were taken out of context from my letters. Lily took her word, and I mean, I guess I understand why. I did mess things up for her and Sal. Oh, there's so much to tell you, son. I just don't think right now is that time."

Cory had no idea how to respond; the endless romance entanglement between the four of them was, in some way, unbelievable. *How can one small group of people have so much scandal and secrets among them? It's crazy.* "Dad, I need you to hear me when I tell you that I didn't mean for this to happen. I didn't even realize it was happening. But when she and I met last year, it was like we were instantly drawn to each other. We couldn't help it—well, at least I couldn't. She may not feel the same way, and that's okay if she doesn't. But I just couldn't go on and lie to Sara every day for the rest of our lives. It wouldn't be fair to anyone. I know this is not the thing anyone wanted or expected, but it did, and I can't take it back. Quite frankly, I don't want to."

Clay tapped his fingers together and then put his hands on the desk. "Cory, I don't want to see you hurt. You know there's going to be a lot of talk and whispers everywhere you go and that people are going to judge you both, and I can't blame them. You understand all this, right?"

"Yeah, I know. But I don't care. I would rather be happy alone than unhappy in what everyone else wants me to be."

Clay exhaled and leaned back on his chair. "Okay, well, you have to tell your mother. I think she has some suspicions already, but you owe it to her. And you best do it fast. She has dinner tonight with Lily at the hospital, and I am fairly sure that she will be asking her tonight if her suspicions are accurate."

Getting up from the seat, he said, "All right, Pop, thanks for the talk. Wish me luck with Mom." Clay could only laugh.

CHAPTER 26

Lily knew that Ruth had an idea of what was going on and was reluctant to have her come over this week, but she knew it was necessary. She knew that Belle and Cory needed to answer questions that people were going to have. Lily felt incredibly sad for Sara and could only think back to a time that she blocked out of her memory for an exceptionally long time. She did not know personally what she was going through, but she was Belle in this situation many years ago, and Ruth was Sara.

As Ruth got into the car with dinner all packed to go, she sat in the driver's seat before turning the ignition. Staring out the windshield, she started to cry; she was taken back to a time that she swore she would not talk about ever again. Now she was left to decide if she was to stand by her son's decision or to try to talk some sense into him and tell him about what his father put her through so long ago. Wiping her face and composing herself, she backed out of the driveway and headed north up Main Street to the hospital. *For so long, I put those memories behind me. When I saw Lily, I knew it was just a matter of time before they came rushing back like a tidal wave. I am so genuinely happy that she has come back and that she and I are working toward a friendship again, but I'll be damned if the past will come back to ruin yet another relationship. No sir re.*

Pulling into the parking garage, she grabbed the casserole, rolls, and dessert and headed off to the third floor. So many of the workers there got to know her very well, and most were surprised she was married to Chief Richards. He was not very well-liked—respected, but not as well-liked as Chief Davis. Over the years, the rivalry between the two men would get worse and worse; and up until recently, no one understood what caused it and why it continued all these years.

Ruth knew people looked at them all differently now, but she was too much of a lady to let them see it bothered her. Ruth always held her head high, even when she knew that everyone looked at her like they felt sorry for her. She had been in love with Clay for as long as she could remember, and she knew she would marry him one day. When that day came, she was the happiest woman on earth. Some did not share in her joy; some felt sorry for her because they thought he was just using her and that she was second best. Whatever their opinions were, she did not care one bit.

Lily could hear the high heels clicking down the hallway toward her room.

"Knock, knock!" Ruth peeked her head around the door with a huge smile and a hand full of delicious food.

"Well, hello friend!"

Both ladies knew that this was going to get awkward and also knew the importance of the conversation.

"What is that amazing smell, Ruth?"

Ruth started to put the food out on the table and onto plates for serving to her friend. "That, my dear, is my famous turkey tetrazzini casserole, homemade buttermilk biscuits, and well, dessert is a surprise." She was smiling over at her friend.

"Well, it smells divine! I cannot wait to try this."

Ruth placed the plate on the portable table for Lily, and Lily took no time at all to take a bite. "Mmmmmm, this is heavenly, Ruthie. It reminds me of your mama's cooking."

Ruth smiled.

"Wait, is this what she used to make us?"

Ruth nodded her head yes.

"Oh my, this takes me back."

Both ladies went silent for a few minutes while they enjoyed their meal and tried to avoid the inevitable. Lily took another bite and figured she should get the conversation started. "So how's everything?"

Ruth finished chewing and replied, "Well, it's been a little interesting the past few hours. How about for you?"

Lily raised her eyebrows and exhaled. "I guess it is safe to assume you spoke with your son?"

"Yes, he came by today and shared some interesting news with us. Sara called off the wedding."

Lily knew this already and did not want to keep any more secrets. "Yes, I heard. And I know my Belle is a part of this whole thing as well."

"Lily, what are we gonna do? You know how this town talks. Shoot, they are still talking about how sad they all feel for me. After three decades of being married to that man, you would think they would see that I love him and I don't care what they say."

"Listen, I feel the same way. However, I know that they are all adults and need to make their own decisions. I do not agree with it, but I will support whatever it is they all decide."

"How can you say that? This will ruin him, his future, his reputation. All because he wants to fulfill some strange fantasy he has. It doesn't make any sense. She has children already. She is probably past having a family with someone. She's your daughter. What do you think?"

Lily was extremely insulted by the things Ruth was saying; she was on the verge of asking her to leave but knew that she was saying all these things because she was scared, scared of many things. "I know this. Yes, my Belle has kids already. And unfortunately for them, they lost their father, her husband, not too long ago, but this is not something we should meddle in. I understand how upset you are because it is like déjà vu. Believe me, I see that. We have no idea if Belle is done having a family or if Cory even wants to have a family. They are more than grown, Ruth, and we need to step aside and let fate take control."

Ruth knew everything Lily was saying was right, but her heart hurt so much for Sara. "I am sorry, but I know how Sara feels, and you should talk to Belle about us and what happened."

"Let me stop you there. She knows everything. I told her everything shortly after I arrived and ran into Sal for the first time in thirty years. I know your heart breaks for Sara, but she is also a grown woman. We, Ruth, were young girls, eighteen to nineteen years old.

We had no idea what the future held for either one of us. We had no idea that a boy was playing us both for fools. I also know that once I found out about everything, I stopped all communications with him, but he did not with me. I should've told you this at lunch, but he sent me more letters, and I mailed them all back. I did not want to hear what he had to say. You were my best friend, and all I wanted was for him to be out of my life forever. When Belle told me she was moving here, I couldn't catch my breath. We know the Grants were a big family back here, even in my brief time living here, and how she and Nate ended up together and back here where it all started and ended for me, well, I couldn't help but think maybe it was fate." Lily looked at her friend, who was crying, and asked her to come sit on the bed with her.

Ruth got up and sat down.

Lily took her hand in hers. "Ruth, you were truly my best friend. I never ever meant to hurt you. I know I said this already, but I wanted you to hear it one more time." Both women were looking at their hands in each other's. "Now about our children, we have to let them make their own choices."

Ruth interrupted, "But the people are going to talk again. Lily, I just don't know if I can handle it again."

Lily agreed quietly, "Yes, I know, and I agree, but we have to be their supporters. They need us to be that for them right now. Plus, how bad could it be, our kids ending up together? Would that be so bad?" Nudging her hand against Ruth's arm, Lily smiled and extended her arms for a warm hug from her best friend. Ruth happily reciprocated.

"Now what has Cory told you? Because I don't know if he has told you everything."

Ruth immediately started to recite what he said today in her kitchen.

"So he didn't tell you that he has been coming to see me almost every day since my heart attack?"

Shocked, Ruth answered, "Uh, no, he did not. But you didn't either."

"Now, Ruth, he asked me not to say anything to anyone, and you know my loyalty and how strong my word is. I couldn't tell you—or even Belle."

"Fair enough. What did he talk about?"

"I think that's something he should answer. But I will tell you that when you find out some of the things that have happened, you will not be happy. Honestly, you will probably be a bit mad at first, but keep an open mind, okay? The two kids have been intertwined long before they even knew they were."

Ruth knew there was a lot of truth behind that and promised she would keep an open mind when Cory finally decided to talk to her.

"Now let's get on to dessert!" Lily was extremely excited for what Ruth brought this week.

"Sugar-free chocolate lasagna, because the doctor told me I needed to bring you sugar-free desserts from now on."

Rolling her eyes, Lily took the plate from Ruth and took a bite, surprised. "Wow, that's actually really good."

"I knew you would like it. I asked the doctor if I could replace the refined sugars with natural, like fruits, and he said yes. So I tweaked my recipe a little bit, and voilà, magnifique!" She took her fingers and kissed them as if she were an Italian chef from black-and-white movies.

CHAPTER 27

Never did I imagine I would be here. This is not the life I pictured for myself and the kids. How is this even fair? Nate and I were supposed to grow old together. I don't know if I will ever be able to move on from him fully. What do I do now? This is not supposed to be happening with Cory. He is engaged to be married to Sara, just a sweet soul. Why? Belle was having an extremely tough time with everything happening right now. *I guess I need to talk to people before they all find out from someone else. I need to start with Chief. I cannot even pretend to assume what he will say or think.*

Driving down Troop Lane, just leaving the hospital, she couldn't help but think about every single thing that had happened over the past few years, but more so the current events. She pulled into the driveway so she could run into the house to check on Katie and the kids before she headed back to the station. "Hey, guys! How is the day going?" Belle yelled out as she walked into the kitchen to make a sandwich for lunch.

"Oh, hey, Mom! It's been good. Katie did my nails. Look!" Rose loved when Katie babysat them; she always did so many fun girly things with her.

Belle raved over the color choice, "Oh, I love that blue, Rosebud! Is your brother at the firehouse?"

Katie nodded her head. "Yeah, I dropped him off about an hour ago. I told him I would be back around three thirty to get him so he can be home for dinner."

"Thank you, Katie. I have no idea what I would do without you."

Belle headed out to the car to get back to work, all the while thinking about Cory and the bomb he dropped on her earlier. It had not been quite easy for her since Nate passed away, everyone looking at her with sad, pathetic eyes and so much pity, she thought. Now everyone was going to look at her for being a homewrecker. *Great. This is all I needed. I was minding my own business, not bothering a soul. He had to come in and mess that all up for all of us—me, Sara, him, our families. And our moms were just starting a friendship again. Ugh.*

Pulling into the lot, she saw his truck again, and panic quickly took hold of her. *Oh my god, not again. I think I'm gonna throw up.* Putting the car in park, she sat in the driver's seat for a minute to compose herself before getting out to confront what was about to come her way. *Okay, Belle, you got this, girl.* Opening the door, she half-expected him to be right there waiting for her, but she looked around, and he wasn't. Weirdly, no one was. *Okay.* As she was walking through the lot, her eyes quickly scanned around to see if he was going to come out at any time—still nothing. Continuing on, she walked into the firehouse and could hear voices coming from the engine bay. As she walked closer, she heard him. She rounded the corner and saw him and all the guys standing there, shooting the shit, it seemed.

"Hey." Her tone was confused by this scene.

"Oh, hey, Belle, what's up?" Scotty was, of course, always the sweetest kid and overly excited to see her sometimes.

"Uh, nothing. What's up here?" She pointed to the group of guys and glared at Cory.

"Well, miss, I was just talking to the guys about a few things. Well, to be honest, I was looking for you, and they told me you should be back soon. I wanted to talk about my outburst earlier today, if that would be all right?"

Belle was pretty embarrassed and hated to be put on the spot. Her cheeks turned a nice shade of crimson rose, and she huffed almost. "Sure. But we are not talking here. We can go outside." She turned to walk out and saw that it was raining. *Of course, it's raining.* "Never mind. My office."

Belle walked into her office. "Close the door, please."

Cory stepped in and closed the door behind him. "Belle—"

She interrupted, "How dare you show up here and put me on the spot like this? This is so unfair, Cory." Cory walked toward her; she backed away. "No, don't you dare do that." He inched closer to her. "I mean it. Stop." She knew she didn't want him to, but she also knew that she couldn't keep doing this to herself. "Cory—"

Cory took her hands in his and folded them together. "Belle, listen to me. I am sorry for this morning. I should have never told you like that. It was unfair of me to do that to you. There are things I need to tell you though. I know now is not the best time to do that, and especially not here. So would it be okay if we went for coffee or something so I can explain everything?"

Belle stood there wanting so badly to yell out *yes*, but there were so many thoughts running around her head. Looking up at this beautiful man, seeing his eyes, she knew he was genuine and that whatever it was he needed to tell her meant a lot to him. "I am sorry, Cory, but I can't. You should go."

It stung to his very core to hear her say those words, but he respected her, and so he left as requested. Walking through the engine bay, the guys all hollered, "See ya later," and Cory closed the door behind him.

Belle dropped to her knees and cried a cry she hadn't done in a long time. She was devastated and heartbroken but knew that she needed to do this. He was making the wrong decision, and she knew she had to make it easy for him to walk away. *Oh, Nathan, what did I just do? You always told me that I would know when the right one walks into my life, that I would smile, laugh, cry, and hurt. And I am now. Is that it? Am I supposed to just run after him?*

Some time passed, and the department was dispatched to an accident with injuries reported, three vehicles, one on its roof, possible entrapment. Belle went white as a ghost and felt ill again, but not the same way she did earlier; this was different. It was almost as if she knew something was wrong. She ran out of her office, and all the guys were moving faster than normal. "Guys, where's this call at?" she yelled out.

Steve hollered back, "It's at the intersection of Main and Carol Drive."

Belle knew that intersection, and it was a dangerous one.

"Belle." Jillian rushed over to her. "It's Captain Richards."

Her heart sank; she felt weak and nearly fainted. "I'm coming with you." She bolted to the back of the ambulance.

The roads were slick; the rain caused thin sheets of black ice everywhere. She was staring through the front when she could finally see the scene.

"Belle, when you get out, please just wait by the ambulance, okay?" Jillian requested.

She nodded her head yes and hopped out of the back. It was so hard for her to see what was going on because it was utter chaos. She jumped in front of the ambulance so she could hear what was happening and see if she could get a better view. As she stood on the step rail, she saw the silver pickup truck and began sobbing. *No, no, no, no, not this man too. I can't lose another one. And the last thing I said to him. This is my fault. I have to go get to him.* She got back out of the ambulance and started her way closer to the scene. As she approached, she could see a small sedan on its roof and a man panicking to get out, the firefighters trying to calm him down to no avail. She looked to the left and could see an SUV with the rear end completely mangled and pushed in toward the back. Looking past that, she saw the silver pickup. It did not seem to have much damage, but she could only see the passenger side.

Trying to navigate where everyone was, she still could not locate him. *Please let him be okay.* Crying and worried, she continued to immerse herself further into the scene until she finally saw him. Like a statue, she stood there, tears pouring down her cheeks; she placed her hands over her nose and mouth and began to sob.

Cory looked up at that exact moment and sprinted to her just as she was falling. "I got you."

She fell into him at that moment and let herself fall completely. "I am so sorry. I was so scared when I heard the call come in. I knew it was you. I felt it."

Smiling down at her, wiping the tears and rain away, he said, "It wasn't me though. I was in the right place at the right time, that's all." Cory's truck was perfectly fine; he was driving out of Karen's and witnessed the accident happen.

"Why did they say three vehicles involved then?"

"Most likely because multiple people called and saw my truck so assumed I was involved too."

Standing there in that moment, with the sheer chaos and icy rain happening all around them, they stared into each other's eyes, and everything else just disappeared. He took his hands, placed them on the side of her cheeks, and leaned down and kissed her.

ABOUT THE AUTHOR

Kit Spayd is about to take the world by storm with her manuscripts. Living on the outskirts of Philly, she grew up in a very close-knit part of her small town where she was graced with the talent to write for all of us to enjoy.

She is a wife, mom, lover, and daughter. She is believed to have superpowers (unknown as of yet), has a few rescue pets, and owns a bakery near her hometown. She started her first manuscript about fifteen years ago, but life happened, and she had to put the pen down for some time to focus on family life.

Sadly, she lost her mom in early 2021, and she returned to writing after this tragic event in her life. Writing was Kit's way of coping with the grief of losing her mom; this loss has also helped to form a special bond with her dad, a Vietnam veteran who is enjoying his retired life as best he can and Kit's biggest fan!

A Delco native, you can find Kit decorating cakes, volunteering with her business at community events, and enjoying her shows. She is a Libra who does not enjoy long walks on the beach but will sit by a roaring firepit on a cool fall evening, has a love for all things horror, and is an avid reader of a variety of genres. She is confident that everyone who reads her books will come back looking for more.

CPSIA information can be obtained
at www.ICGtesting.com
Printed in the USA
BVHW081925060723
666786BV00006B/205